BETWEOS

Ken McConnell

ALSO BY KEN MCCONNELL

The Star Saga

GB Press

B E T W E O S

First Edition: January 2026
ISBN: 978-1-969784-13-2

Cover art by Byron McConnell

Author's website: ken-mcconnell.com

"Only the dead have seen the end of war."
- Plato

Elysia

1

All that I've ever wanted to do was kill bugs. Since I was old enough to carry a toy rifle, I was blasting those nasty creatures in my imagination. Maybe I was just reenacting what I saw in the holograms or pretending to be my war hero grandfather. Either way, I knew I was born to fight. Born to kill them like some angry god of war from antiquity. I knew I was destined for glory on the battlefields of Betweos. I just had to get there first.

I waited my entire childhood for the war.

When I was finally old enough, it was my time. Nothing could stop me or save those wretched aliens from my wrath. The funny thing about life is that it never happens as you thought it would. Wars never quite go how you expect them to, either. It turns out the first victim of war is the truth.

My parents, of course, fiercely objected to me joining the army. They wanted me to enter the agriculture business, as was the family tradition. Try as I might, I couldn't see myself as being a farmer for the rest of my life. I just didn't have the temperament for it. I craved adventure and danger. I could find neither of those things in business. I could only really find them in the army.

We called them bugs or segs, but technically, they were sentient insects or entos. They evolved on the planet Acheron, which orbited Suth Two, the red dwarf star of our binary star system. Suth One was a middle-aged yellow star around my homeworld of Elysia orbited. There were five planets in the

Suth One system and three in the Suth Two system. Then
there was Betweos. So named because it orbited both stars in
an odd, figure-eight pattern. Once every human generation
the wandering gas giant and its coven of moons crossed over
and around one star only to pass over again to orbit the
second star.

I know it's complicated. In secondary school, my science
teacher assured me that Betweos's orbit was quite impossible,
yet there it was, wandering between the two stars. Every
generation, we sent soldiers to the midpoint of its orbit to
fight for control of the three major moons of Betweos. It was
critical to gain control of them before Betweos passed around
our star so that the segs couldn't use them to attack our home
world. The opposite was true when the gas giant swung back
around and headed closer to Acheron. In the orbit before my
grandfather's campaign, the segs used the moons of Betweos
to stage raids on our crops. They always went after our food
for some reason.

The Bug War has been raging for at least three
generations now. My grandfather, Jarna, fought in the first
major skirmish between the Acheron and Elysian armies on
the moons of Betweos. His leadership and combat bravery
helped maintain Elysian dominance when Betweos swung
around to our side of the binary system. The entos were
vanquished then, but they would return to fight again, and we
lost control of the precious real estate when the gas giant
moved back around the red star.

My father's generation lost control of the moons as
Betweos headed back around the bug star. Not that my father
had much to do with that campaign. Joros served on the
transfer ships and never even saw actual combat. His general
disinterest in the war and in having me go off to fight was
rooted in the fact that he hadn't lived up to Jarna's legendary
reputation as a war hero. His was the only generation that had
lost control of the Betweos moons. Growing up, I always
imagined that it was my duty to return the family's good
name by becoming an even better soldier than my
grandfather had been.

When I was eight years old, I used to go fishing with my

grandfather up in the mountains. We would cast lines in the icy river and he would tell me his war stories. He always made it seem like combat was the noblest of adventures. I came away believing that fighting in the bug war was the greatest thing a person could do for his planet. My grandfather was convinced that if the buggers ever won, they would take over our lush planet and exterminate everyone.

I was steeped in my grandfather's near-mythic lore, and I yearned to wear the sky blue and white colors of the Elysian army. I wanted nothing more than to drop into combat with the infamous First Platoon, First Field Army, the same unit my grandfather served in.

My love for my grandfather ran deep in me and sometimes exceeded my love for my father. Although I would never admit that, it was undeniably true. When Jarna passed away, I was just sixteen years old. Seeing him laid out in his coffin upset me more than anything else I had ever experienced. We shouldn't have to witness the passing of our heroes. In my dreams, I often saw Jarna walking into the mountain mists, fading away like an old soldier. In time, those dreams faded away, too.

I secretly enlisted in the Elysian Army on my eighteenth birthday. A month later, when it was time for me to go through basic military training, I told my parents I was attending a college prep school, which they wanted for me. When I returned, I had to wait another few months before shipping out. I spent the time working in the fields with my childhood friends.

On my last workday on Elysia, I raced my best friend Hector back from the fields. We always made work into a competition. Racing ag-skiffs over fields of gold for nothing more than bragging rights was a metaphor for our relationship. He always beat me. Sometimes, he'd plan his entire day's work just to end closer to the shop to get a leg up on me. Other times, he would modify his skiff's engine to give him just enough power to beat me in a dead heat. Most of the time, I just waved off his boasting. He was six months younger than me and, as a result, would never beat me to the war.

I honestly tried to win our last race together. I picked the fastest skiff, and I had the shortest route back. When his call came over the comms, I was on the ground, scanning an ear of corn for the sounds of chlorophyll. Chemical reactions sang their healthy tunes in my earpiece as sunlight glinted off the SVK corporate logo on the scanner.

"Hey, shucker boy, I'm heading in. This is your last chance to beat me," Hector's irritating voice taunted.

I tossed the ear of corn and climbed up the pole ladder into the flat glass-covered cockpit of my ag-skiff. "You're on," I replied.

It took me seconds to gear up the throttle and retract the pole. I was careening over the tassels at full throttle in no time. The poor ag-skiff's engine labored away as I pushed it faster than it had ever gone before. The sensation of speed flying low over the crops always made it seem like we were moving, but in reality, we were not going that fast at all.

Workers on the platforms watched us get closer and, no doubt, cheered for Hector to win. I was still well ahead of him. A smile spread over my lips. I was finally going to win this stupid race.

"Attention approaching vehicles. Please decrease your speed immediately," the dispatcher warned us.

I opened my mic and blew a raspberry into it. I didn't give a damn about company policy on my last day. Hector was still way behind me, and I would beat him.

That's when the stalk monkey leaped out of nowhere, swinging its way right into my path. I had to swerve hard or hit the furry creature. They normally had sense enough to avoid ag-skiffs, but this one darted right into my path. Only my quick reflexes saved it from getting killed.

The sudden change in direction caused my skiff to flutter and dip into the crops, where it sheered off tassels and slowed me just enough to let Hector get out in front. He laughed and made a silly face at me as he passed, just like a spoiled little brat.

Hector again coasted into victory while I limped back to the platform with a damaged grill and a bruised ego. Cheering workers formed around Hector's skiff as it landed on spindly skids. I set my smoking and clattering ag-skiff down for a landing; it sighed like an overworked mule.

Shutting my craft down, I joined the crowd around Hector and reluctantly offered my hand to the winner. He shook it firmly and tried, but failed, to hold back his pride. "Sorry, old buddy, but you know I just hate to lose."

"Some people live a charmed life," I said.

He turned back to the crowd and shouted, "Undefeated!"

I brushed off his braggadocios comment and let him have his moment. Tomorrow, I'll head off to war, and he'll still be racing ag-skiffs on the farm.

We made our way back to the dispatch to turn in our recorders. As we checked them in, the dispatcher overheard me talking about leaving the next day for orbit. "We're supposed to spend a day or two on the way station. Our transfer ship is still being replenished," I said.

"You won't find glory in the war, only deception and death," the dispatcher said in her terse, earthy voice. Hector and I looked at her strangely for a moment and then shrugged. She was probably just jealous that she wasn't shipping out, too.

"Jered, what ship are you taking?" Hector asked.

"The *Elpida*."

Hector's eyes shined. He wanted to be going with me, and it was no doubt killing him he wasn't.

"That's the one Rickover took in *Victor's Way*. Now that was a show!"

I nodded in complete agreement. Between us, we had seen every holodram about the Bug War ever, and that said something. They created more military dramas in anticipation of the current conjunction than in the war's history. There were historical shows about past campaigns and fictional looks into future battles with hardware and weapons that were only in dreams now. More young people were volunteering to enlist than ever before. It was a banner year for recruiters, and the central government couldn't have been happier. It also helped that more and more soldiers were coming home alive thanks to better-designed defensive systems.

Some people called the Bug War a Suit War, where heavily armored humans took on the Acheron entos in faceplate-to-faceplate single-combat skirmishes. Nobody hides inside armored vehicles anymore. They deemed it too costly to risk killing ten people when a single armored vehicle got hit. One highly mobile and armored suit warrior could do more damage than a single tank and cover more ground doing it. Today's war was about real estate on the three largest moons of Betweos. So far, the entos had not held ground when the gas giant came around our star. I aimed to keep it that way when I got to the front.

Since my grandfather's generation, no humans have survived the journey around Suth One. My father's generation tried but failed. Cut off from resupply ships and facing increasing attacks from the bugs, they just couldn't make the long journey and bailed out before Betweos was too far away to make it home. The primary thrust of the current battle was to augment our forces enough to make such a journey and strike at the heart of the bug planet, Acheron. I was proud to be a part of this attack wave. Hector would join me in a few months, and we would be on the greatest military advance in the war's history. We were convinced that we could win this war this time.

Hector and I had been in love with the same girl since we were kids. I saw it in his eyes whenever we were all together. Trille had always favored me over him, which irritated him more than he ever let on. I knew he loved her because I loved her for all the same reasons. She was beautiful, smart, and caring. All traits that caused any red-blooded male to become sick with desire for her. Her golden curls hung gently over her soft shoulders, and she walked with a sway that enticed a young man's fancy. She wasn't always so beautiful to us, but as we all blossomed, she bloomed the brightest.

I was going to marry Trille when I got back from war. She knew it; I knew it, and so did Hector. It was only a matter of time. Time was something I was soon to be very short of, as I was shipping out in the morning. Trille met us at the monorail station as we stepped off the ramp. She wore a white dress, and her smile radiated her happiness at seeing us both.

"So, who won the last race, guys?" she asked, throwing her arms around my neck and kissing me. Hector raised his hand with a self-righteous grin on his face. Trille and I separated, and Hector reached out to shake my hand. It would be the last time we saw each other until he arrived at Betweos. "Don't end the war before I get there," he said.

"I can't promise that, my friend."

He patted my shoulder and went with a wink and a nod to Trille. She watched him leave and then turned to me. "I couldn't wait for this day to end," she whispered.

Me either.

Elysia

2

Trille's studio apartment was small but cozy. Her mattress dominated the main room before picture windows that looked out at the glittering luxury of the city. We had spent most of our time in her bed leading up to my departure. On our last night together, we were quiet and reflective. She kissed me with her soft lips and guided me to sit on the bed. Then she said, "I have a gift for you, soldier."

She produced a tightly wrapped, triangular bundle of blue fabric from underneath her pillow—the Elysian flag. She placed it in my hands and kissed me again.

"I know it's old-fashioned, but I want you to keep it and think of me when you see it," she said, unfolding the flag and wrapping it around us like a blanket.

We spent the evening making love under the flag. When morning came, I quietly got up and put on my dress blues. My bag was packed and ready to go by the door. I returned to the bed as Trille woke up with a stretch. Her blonde hair was golden in the sunlight, streaming through the buildings outside. She sat up, and the flag fell loosely around her bare shoulders. I slid off a golden ring from my left hand and put it gently into her open palm.

"This ring belonged to my grandfather. He won it for conspicuous bravery in the face of the enemy. My father wore it during his tour, and it protected him from danger. I want you to keep it until I return. A placeholder for our love."

Trille cried. She knew how much the family heirloom

meant to me, and she couldn't believe I was giving it to her like this. I slid the golden band over her finger, surprising her again.

"Will you marry me, Trille?"

She wiped the tears from her eyes and wrapped her arms around my neck.

"Of course I will."

"Let this be my promise to you that I will return and make you my wife," I said.

I did not doubt I would return and make good on my promise. My confidence was so great that it seemed to quiet her tears. She stood up, and we folded the flag back into a triangle. Standing naked in my arms, she hugged me tightly.

"I love you, Jered. Please come back to me."

"I will."

***

Morning commuters flooded the streets of Ornos as I made my way downtown. I looked around at the faces that passed me. Most of them stared back at me with some level of respect and gratitude in their eyes. Where I was heading and what I was about to do, I was doing for them. I was a soldier, and soon, I would kill the enemy so that these people could live in peace and prosperity. All around me, plastered on the walls of the buildings, were government recruiting posters showing idyllic young people wearing the sky blue army uniform with big, bold smiles on their shiny faces. My heart was heavy with pride, and my footsteps lighter, knowing I was about to leave this world for the adventure of a lifetime.

Then I saw my father's face ahead and crashed back to reality. He didn't look angry or even surprised to see me in uniform. He looked like he had expected to find his son here, about to board a transfer shuttle to orbit.

"Your mother's going to die when I tell her where you are," he said.

I lowered my eyes, ready for the inevitable scolding I was about to receive. My only solace was knowing that I was of legal age now, and there was nothing my father could say to me that would stop me from going to war.

"Don't tell her," I offered.

Joros shook his head. "I couldn't do that to her."

"How did you know I'd be here?" I asked.

My father sighed and looked around at the other blue-uniformed individuals heading uptown. "I did the same thing to my parents."

I sure as hell didn't expect the man to say that. After all, my grandfather was a legendary war hero of the family. Surely, he approved of his son following in his footsteps.

"I thought grandfather wanted you to fight?"

Joros shook his head slowly. "He did everything in his power to stop me from going. I was young and naïve, just like you are now. Nothing would stop me from being a hero like he had become. I signed up for Suit Soldier, just like he had done. It wasn't until I was in space that I discovered I would stay on the transfer ships. The great Jarna's influence in the army was still pretty powerful back then, and he'd gotten my orders changed."

I stared back at my father and saw the pain in his eyes.

"Why didn't he want you to follow in his footsteps?"

"Because he knew there was a damn good chance I'd be killed or maimed. He understood how badly I wanted to prove myself in combat. But he also knew he needed me to help him with the family business. If I didn't come home, there would be no legacy to pass down to his grandkids and great-grandchildren."

"Were you disappointed when you couldn't fight?"

Joros shoved his hands into his pockets and nodded. "I was."

"What did you do?"

"I endured the taunts of my buddies as they went off to fight while the son of Jarna stayed on the ship. It was humiliating, but I returned home and learned everything I could from my father about business. Over time, the company thrived, and I eventually had a son."

I saw the circle of life more clearly now. Jarna had always trained me to be the best possible hunter. I assumed it was because he wanted me to do well in the next campaign. He wanted me to continue the family legend my father had allowed to be tarnished; now I saw he was training me because he knew I would have to fight, and he wanted me to be a survivor. All my life I had thought my father had chosen not to fight in the war. I thought he was ambivalent to the cause. I even thought he was a coward. Now that I knew the truth, I felt enormous love for him.

"I will come back, Father," I said as I stepped forward and embraced him. "I promise."

He patted my back as he gripped me tightly. Then he let go and went on his way, looking over his shoulder once. Was that pride on his face or fear? I believed it was pride.

**

I arrived at the spaceport a few minutes early and used the extra time to visit the war memorial nearby. I knew the giant statue well and wanted to find my grandfather's cylinder before I left. The statue was a twice-life-size depiction of two early war Elysian soldiers defending themselves from an overwhelming advance of more alien bugs. Their backs were to each other, and they were firing on an enemy that had them surrounded. The pose was as familiar to every citizen of Elysia as the blue and white colors of our flag. The scene was reenacted in war dramas and paintings and printed on our currency.

I remember playing war games with Hector and other friends as kids. We always recreated this famous pose, pretending to blast enemy bugs with our rubber band guns. It was a good time.

My eyes scanned the polished black marble sides of the monument where all the cylinders were placed. Each contained a small portion of the ashes of those who had made the supreme sacrifice. I knew just where to look to find Jarna's golden cap. It was inscribed with my grandfather's name, serial number, and regiment. It was one of many thousands of such gold and silver caps that surrounded the monument. I stared at the cap and then closed my eyes. I will make you proud, grandfather.

A commotion got my attention, and I turned to see war protesters moving around the monument. They were a motley group of civilians holding signs that read "Bug Myth," "Go Home," and "Peace Not War." They were a small and vocal part of society that refused to see any value in why we fought the bugs.

Another young man in uniform instinctively approached me as if there were strength in numbers. "What's going on?" I asked him.

"Some kind of Peacer rally. I don't understand how they can demonstrate here, of all places." The man was larger than me and had dark hair and eyes. "Name's Saburo," he offered.

"Jered. These people make me sick just looking at them," I said.

Saburo turned to look at me closer. "Say, you're not related to Jarna of the famous B1 raid, are you?"

I had to smile; it wasn't every day that someone asked me that. Despite how much of a legend my grandfather once was, it was ancient history to most people.

"Yes, he was my grandfather."

Saburo shook my hand. "Well, I'll be. Are you shipping out today?"

I nodded.

"It's an honor to serve with you, Jered, grandson of the famous Jarna."

The crowd let out a harsh chant against the military. Saburo looked at them with disgust and said, "Come on, we'd better get back to the spaceport before I do something I'll regret."

I felt the same way. It would not be good to get in a fight before we even had the chance to get on the shuttle. We made our way past the crowd with balled fists.

I noticed that many of the protesters were actual veterans. They wore gray shirts with unit patches from previous campaigns. I couldn't understand why veterans were protesting the war. They should be unit representatives for the recruiters, not gathering in public to denounce the bug war. Dressed like vagrants, with long, stringy hair and dirty, ragged clothes. Then I noticed the disabled veterans, missing legs and arms. I had never seen that side of war before, and it was more than a little unsettling.

One protester stepped in front of Saburo and me. When we tried to go around him, he countered, limping on what was an artificial leg. The man was not much older than we were. His eyes had a hard, distant look to them.

"Hey everybody, look at the fresh meat. All dressed up for the butcher shop."

Other veteran protesters surrounded us while the crowd continued singing peace songs. Saburo eyed them all wearily, as did I.

"Go home, boys. The war is nowhere for you to grow up," a second protester pleaded.

She wore an old army overcoat with the sleeve tied in a knot where her left arm used to be. She wore a red headband with Bug Myth printed on it in white. The other protesters had similar headbands that spoke of ending the war. They were carrying Peacer flags with three-colored spheres on a black background.

Saburo and I took a defensive posture with our backs to each other. We slowly edged our way through the crowd, enduring taunts and jeers aimed at the military. I made eye contact with a striking young woman with silver hair, dressed in rags and singing a peace anthem. She looked right through me with her dark eyes, and in a moment, she was gone. The crowd moved on and let us leave. I didn't know who she was, but I knew I would never forget her haunting face.

***

The atmosphere around the military spaceport was decidedly more friendly than the crowd at the memorial. We were rounded up and organized into groups by soldiers wearing starched and pressed dress uniforms. Saburo and I fell into line with other recruits and were slowly in-processed. I was so impressed with the regal uniforms and the professionalism of the people wearing them. Some were veterans, and many were only a few years older than we were. I marveled at their ribbons and shiny belt buckles and their shoes polished to mirror-like perfection. It inspired me to be just like them when I returned.

They took us into fitting rooms where our space suits were assigned. They were probably the most expensive thing we would wear until we got our armor. The fabric was made from a composite material with sections that could shrink over missing limbs to maintain suit integrity. I tried not to think of that ever happening to me. Each suit was adjusted and calibrated to very tight tolerances. The procedures for wearing them were intimidating, especially if you overthought what could happen to you while wearing the suit.

It was afternoon before we finally began boarding the transport. I was tired and aching for something to eat. There would be no in-flight meal on this trip into the micro-gravity of space. Too many recruits had tossed their cookies when they reached orbit, so you had to wait until you were docked to the way station to eat.

The transfer shuttles were tall, thin rockets with stubby-winged space planes at the top for reentry into the atmosphere. I had watched them launching for months now from out in the fields. The long, white contrails that cut into the clear blue skies always made me yearn to be on them. I was finally getting my chance to ride the column of smoke into space and beyond.

The acceleration we felt when taking off was exhilarating. We were pressed back into our seats so much that our safety belts felt loose. The launch took just minutes to get us into space but stretched to hours to get us up to our required orbit. I was lucky enough to get a window seat and was mesmerized by the view of Elysia from low orbit. It was such a beautiful world, and I was honored to be chosen to defend her.

I looked across the aisle and saw that some people had colorful face masks from puking into them. A few rows behind me, I noticed a woman staring at me. It was the woman's dark eyes and droll expression from the peace rally. What the hell was she doing here? Why would a Peacer even want to fight in a war they were protesting? There was no need for a draft, as more than enough volunteers signed up to fight. She looked away from me and I turned back around too. Maybe she felt differently about the war than her family and friends did. Perhaps she was rebelling by choosing to fight instead of protesting. Either way, I had no interest in learning her story. I was newly engaged to my childhood sweetheart and had no business looking at anyone else.

There was much more to learn about my fellow soldiers and fighting before we reached Betweos. I stared out the porthole at the shimmering stars and felt relieved to finally be living out my lifelong dream of becoming a warrior. The future was before me now, like a blank slate. I briefly wondered if I had the metal to be the best. Would I even make it through training? Deep inside, I knew I would succeed. I would not waste a lifetime of waiting for this moment. There was no turning back now.

Acheron

3

I've always hated the lower classes. The lower I go in search of food, the more I despise the people living down there. They have plenty of food, they have working technology, and they have their freedom. The RUTs never come for their children and take them away. They don't have to beg or steal for food, and death is something that only happens after they've lived a long life.

If it were up to me, I would never again descend to their levels.

But I have no choice. I'm the tribe's leader, and my duty is to care for, protect, and feed them. So, I descend into the lower classes and take all I can from them. Today's pilfering only resulted in a few ears of flint corn that I hid in my long jacket as I ascended a dark, dank stairwell. The lifts only work up to three levels from the surface. From there on, I have to walk. Each time I descend to scavenge for food, I risk not being able to even climb back to the surface where I live. Everything mechanical has rusted beyond use down to the third level of the planet. Fortunately for me, concrete stairwells take much longer to crumble in the heavy acid rains from the surface.

Water makes it down this far, and everything gets covered in moss and fungus. The gutter rats and other vermin from the lower levels die out, the closer I get to the surface. Nothing lives on the surface of my world except human trash —castoffs from the elite society below. Most of us are under eighteen because when we make it to adulthood, the RUTs take us, and we never return.

RUTS or Round Up Troops are the goons that work for the Arachian government. They scour the surface, snatching people up to fight in a war they're fighting in space. That's the rumor, anyway; hell, who knows? It could just be an elaborate cover for something equally bizarre. Never trust the RUTs.

On the second level, I tore open a hidden stash comprising an old trooper rifle and a rain slicker with a breather mask. One can't survive on the surface without them. I heard thunder booming from above. The acid rain leaves a dark red stain on the steps of the stairwell. The rain that burns. If exposed, it leaches into you and oozes into the scabs. Everyone on the surface has the mark of blood rain somewhere on their body. Get too much of it, and you become infertile and weak-minded. They say it's the result of runaway pollution from the machinery of the lower classes. I believe them. I've seen the stacks and the columns of black death pouring into the air. My hatred runs very deep.

As I pushed outside, the rain drizzled, and I could smell sulfur. My slicker flapped in the wind as I ran with the rifle close to my torso—black splotches on the gray slicker aided in hiding me from the eye, both human and machine.

A patch of thick fog obscured the first trench I came to. I made this trip many times before and knew when my feet would give out under me. I rolled to a stop against the far wall of the rusted metal trench. RUTs were nearby. My motion alarm vibrated as soon as I stopped. While I was underground, it shielded me from them, but on the surface, I became fair game for their sensors.

I crawled along the pit, carefully staying as low as possible, and pulled out my handheld scanner. It keyed off their metallic red armor and calculated how many were present and from which direction they were approaching. RUTs relied solely on their technology; if you could trick their sensors, they wouldn't even see you if you stood before them. Fools.

I stood up and swung the flat barrel of my rifle at the

nearest targets. A few pulls of the trigger and scorching plasma bolts cut through the fog toward the approaching troopers. I pulled the rifle down before they could return fire. Ejecting the power clip, I replaced it with a fuse, toggle switch, and numerical readout. I flipped the toggle to arm it and then wrapped the rifle in tape with tiny metal flechettes. Gunny had taught us how to turn rifles into frags. I loved that kid.

I slipped away down another bend in the trench and felt the ground shake as the rifle exploded and killed a RUT stupid enough to have picked it up. The death would trigger more troopers to the area, so I had to press on.

Making my way through rusted industrial wastelands— the hollowed remains of a bygone industrial society—I finally arrived on my home turf. My tribe lived inside the remains of a food processing factory one level down from the actual surface. Our ancestors built on top of the older cities, creating layers of machinery like strata of sedimentary rock. At some point, they had extinguished the planet's ecology and had to go subterranean to avoid the toxic air of the surface.

Geros, the oldest man in my tribe, could read the writing we found in printed books. His knowledge of the past was limited to whatever we could find for him to read. Most of it was instructional manuals for mechanical devices that would never run again. Sometimes, he read our stories on a mythical planet where the air was breathable and the rain didn't burn us. He said it was Acheron before the turning under. Rubbish.

My trench tribe was the Roofers. It referenced that we inhabited the roof of a society that lived largely in the world's basement. There were about a dozen of us in total. Most were kids. A few adults were too weak to be taken by the RUTs, and a few elders were too frail to be useful. There were a handful of older kids, myself included, who searched for food and waged a guerrilla war on the RUTs.

Stepping inside the darkened inner sanctum of the factory, Grim greeted me. Slik was wiry, with greasy brown hair and a mean streak. Grim was a short, distempered kid, more animal than human. Grim had the strange but fortunate ability to tell when someone was approaching and reacted by hopping around on all fours and barking like a dog. He was our sentry and spent much of his time alone at the entrance.

I handed Grim a piece of flint corn, and he quickly snatched it from my hand. Then he did a tight circle before settling down and eating it.

Slik clasped my hand as I removed my mask.

"He's been all worked up like that ever since 'ya left," he said, motioning to Grim.

I sat beside the grubby kid and petted his back as he ate. He calmed down with my touch. I looked up at Slik. "Patrols are coming. I downed a few getting back."

Slik shook his head and sighed. "Early this month."

Grim stopped gnawing on the corn and whispered, "We go now."

***

Gunny ran the armory. A kid with a perpetually dirty face, he took his job as seriously as any adult would. He spent his days polishing gun barrels, building frags, and assembling deadly weapons from broken and spare parts found in the miles of tunnels. Nobody messed with him after they realized he was as good a shot with a scattergun as he was cleaning one. I handed Gunny a foil-wrapped bar, and his dark eyes shined. He may have worked like an adult, but I paid him in candy. He quickly devoured the chocolate, adding to the dirt collage on his face. I never liked sweets, but if it meant satisfying my armorer, there's no depth I wouldn't descend to find him candy.

Gunny saved the best of his weapons for me.

He handed me his latest prized possession: an extremely lethal plasma rifle. I inspected the weapon, admiring the blued metal and the rails for mounting scopes and scanners. I smiled as I hefted it and took aim at an imaginary trooper. Gunny licked chocolate from his lips and smacked them. "Nothing but the best for you, Gaven. This one's power-to-range ratio is unmatched," Gunny said.

"You're worth all the candy on the planet, Gunny."

Slik took the next best rifle and jammed energy packs into it. I could tell he wanted the new rifle by how he eyed it as he checked over his weapon. Grim always used the shortest barrel pistol he could find. He carried it in a holster around his barrel chest, leaving his hands free to crawl around and into crevices.

Slik and I were the hunters of our trench tribe. It was strictly a boy's club, though. No girls were allowed to be hunters. They were too highly prized as breeders to risk getting blown up or captured by the RUTs. That didn't stop some girls from trying to join us in defense of the tribe. Shen was one such girl. Before the scabs got her, she was an okay, if somewhat shy, tribe member. She stuck with the elders, tending to their needs, even before her own. Once she contracted the scabs, though, she became quite a fighter. Challenging Slik and me repeatedly for the right to attack the RUTs with us.

I appreciated her enthusiasm. However, she had no combat training and was more of a liability than an asset. We always left her behind when we went out hunting, and tonight would be no different, as far as Slik and I were concerned.

Shen ran into the room and jumped on my back, her arms holding onto me for dear life. A strained voice cracked in my ear. "Take me with you, Gaven. Please!"

Slik reached over and pulled her off of me, slamming her against a wall of the makeshift armory.

She stared ruthlessly at him through her stringy brown hair. I continued filling my pockets with ammo clips and frags like fruit at an unattended market below. Slik took a disliking to Shen the first time she started pestering us to go on hunts. By now, he was good and tired of her shenanigans. He held her hard against the wall until she stopped squirming to get loose.

"We ain't got time for this now. RUTs have come early, you hear?" Slik asked.

She spat in his face, and I turned around in time to see him raise an arm to her. I caught his arm. "Let her go. She can come this time. We'll need all the distractions we can get today."

Slik relented, but not before wiping off her saliva and kneeing her in the gut. Shen bent over, trying to catch her breath. Then she stood defiantly and said, "I don't want to live like this anymore. Let me die with some dignity, defending the tribe."

Slik grabbed some frag tape, pulled it out, and wrapped it around her waist. I realized what he was doing about the same time as Shen and stopped him. She took my hand and implored me to let him continue. I looked into her pained eyes. I knew that she'd been suffering with the scabs and that she wasn't long for this life. Still, it didn't feel right to turn her into a human bomb. "Let him do it. I want to take as many of those bastards as I can."

I had to admire her determination, even if I hated the result. I turned away. We'd never had a human frag as a weapon before, and I had no plan on how to use one. Slik continued taping explosives to her body. She could only carry so much weight before she couldn't keep up with us. I suddenly got a dreadful feeling this was not going to go well for any of us.

***

As we advanced, we set out along a familiar trench line, checking our markers for RUT activity. Shen was lagging, forcing Slik to go back and pull her along so she wouldn't slow down our progress. She didn't have a rain slicker, but she had a breather mask. No goggles meant she could barely see where she was going in the driving rain. The weight of her explosive load was slowing her progress, and I could sense that Slik's patience with her was dwindling.

I didn't know what I was going to do with her. She was wired with enough explosives to take out a lander craft, so using her to take out a handful of troopers was not ideal. Using her as a weapon at all turned my stomach. Although she was ready to die, I knew I could never allow that to happen. She was one of us, and as their leader, they charged me with protecting all my people, not just the healthy ones.

I ducked into a tangle of rotted tree roots to enter a tunnel below the surface for a stretch. How many trees could live and find root in all this man-made material was beyond me. Their gnarly gray limbs were devoid of leaves and sometimes mistaken for people on the surface. Gunny said they had adapted to find nutrients in the oils and carbon-based elements inside long-rusted machinery.

I looked back the way I had come and only saw Slik approaching me.

"Where is she?" I shouted.

"Let's leave her here, the scroach is slowing us down," Slik whined. "You can't save everyone, you know. Sometimes, you have to learn to let them go!"

I ignored him and ran back to find Shen.

She was struggling to get over a trench wall, standing in ankle-deep sludge. As I approached, I watched her struggle to lift a leg over the wall. My motion alarm buzzed, and I instinctively stopped and got low under my slicker. She saw me go down and did the same.

Sometimes, you could hear the RUTs moving over the ground, their armored suits clanging over the metal landscape. They moved across the planet as if they owned it. As if nothing we did could harm them. I told Slik it was part of their terror tactics to scare us out of our caves. Once we learned just to hunker down and wait, they usually moved on empty-handed.

I waited, trusting the IR fooling pattern of my slicker to keep me unseen by their suit sensors. My patience was rewarded once again. The patrol had changed directions and moved on. I slowly slipped to the trench where Shen was squatting in a cold, wet puddle.

I reached down with my arm, and she took it. She was heavier than I expected, but I hoisted her up and over to my level. "Thanks," she breathed.

"Stick close, they are nearby."

I headed back to where Slik was, careful to keep glancing over my shoulder to ensure Shen followed me. She was. The red rain was coming down even harder as we ducted into the vine-covered entrance to the tunnel.

Slik came back and hollered for us to come up to his position. He climbed through what used to be an air duct, just big enough for two. I left Shen to catch her breath and climbed inside with Slik. We could see across a level area where two landing craft were parked. They posted several sentries around them, standard Acheron Army precautions. Slik handed me his binoculars, and I scanned the area. The hairs on my neck rose as I surveyed the weathered gray landers. This wasn't normal. They never parked this close together so that they wouldn't lose two assets if one of them were fragged. It was an unusually arrogant move, even for them.

"This is weird, something's not right," I mumbled.

"What's ever right 'bout roundup?"

"Not that. Something's not right about how this roundup's going," I said.

Slik looked at me with a scrunched brow.

"It's too easy," I stated.

"For us or them?"

A thunderous mechanical boom echoed throughout the landscape, shaking us against each other. I focused back on the landers and saw a personnel carrier on wheels bound over a pile of rubble and come to a stop near one lander. It had a flatbed behind the driver, and there were bodies stacked in the bed. Several troopers came out and started flinging the bodies around the open area. I zoomed the binocs in closer and recognized the inert form of Gunny. A sickening feeling inside made my gut churn.

"Dammit, let's get closer," I said, inching my way back out of the confined space. Slik jumped down after me. "What's wrong? What did you see?"

Shen caught the look in my eyes, and she immediately became scared.

"Let's go now," I said.

We headed down a former sewer system tunnel until it came to a crossroads. I stepped out into the intersection and froze. Two troopers were a few meters away, shining their headlamps down the tunnel at me. I froze. They saw me, but they didn't see me. They saw the bogus signal my scanner was broadcasting of another trooper. I gave them a thumbs up.

"Never mind, he's got 'em," one of the troopers said.

They turned off their lights and moved down another tunnel. I let out my breath slowly. My jamming device allowed me to send bogus signals their scanners picked up. In reality, it was me standing there, plain as day. The trick never failed because the RUTs completely relied on their scanner helmets. They never saw the world as it was, just how it looked through their instruments. Fools.

Knowledge of how their scanners worked was passed down to me by other tribal members, who were far more adept at technology than I was. The one attribute that helped me get by the most was remembering what others had told me. When your tribe was mobile and didn't have any way to pass on knowledge other than verbal communication, those who could recall more survived longer. I never looked at it as anything other than a pure survival instinct.

We continued down the sewer tunnel until it came to another intersection. Several vents made from metal grating probably funneled wastewater long ago but were now just rusting in the acid rain. I kicked one hard, and it broke open. Squatting down, I could see that it let out into an open pit where I had never been before. We could hear the RUTs stomping around in the tunnel behind us.

"Let's go, they're coming this way," Slik urged.

That voice inside of me urged caution again. It always got louder whenever I ventured into unknown territory. Today, I ignored it, opting for a clean getaway instead.

I slipped into the pit and raised my rifle around the perimeter as the others followed close behind me. All I could see was dark, churning storm clouds and drizzle. The pit was empty except for collected pools of rainwater in the corners. Our boots splashed as Slik and I backed each other up with our rifles pointing up. Shen stood in the middle with her eyes lowered to keep the rain out of them. The pit was small. Much smaller than the average room or cave of metal I was familiar with. Something about the size of the pit nagged my inner voice.

The drizzle stopped.

The vent that I had kicked in fell to the ground with a clatter, scaring the crap out of all of us. The ground throbbed as if we were on top of some generator that had mysteriously come alive after being dormant for a lifetime.

"Where are we? What's happening?" Slik asked.

I was familiar with the mechanical sounds of working technology from my many trips below, and this was no different. That empty feeling again in the pit of my stomach. Gunny was dead. The other bodies I had seen were members of my tribe, I was sure of it. Then it hit me. The pit was roughly the same size as a troop carrier.

"We've been drafted," I said.

Slik and Shen stared incredulously at each other and then turned to me. The ground started lifting, forcing us to adjust our stance. Huge metal bay doors started blocking the daylight as they covered the pit from the outside.

We had been chased into a trap that neither of us had ever seen before. I should have listened to that voice in my head.

Slik lost it.

He screamed into the darkness, dropped his rifle, and lunged for Shen. His wet fingers fumbled to find the detonator on her jacket as she helplessly fought him off. I reached between them and shoved Slik off of her. Before he could come back at me, I ripped the detonator off of her and threw it hard against the metal wall, where it shattered.

Slik screamed again in anger as the metal plates slammed shut, casting us into total darkness. For the first time, I felt the weight of the universe closing in on me.

Acheron

4

The troop carrier's darkened interior lit up without warning to reveal a circle of armed RUTs pointing their rifles at us. The ride was bumpy, and I felt the carrier change directions several times as the power increased and lowered. We had placed our weapons, including the explosives that Shen had worn, into a pile behind us. Slik had argued to set them off and remove the whole carrier, but I wasn't ready to die yet.

We slowly raised our hands in surrender, our faces filled with fear and suspicion. A trooper backed up to let a tall man dressed in black with short, spiked red hair come into the circle.

"My name is Polit Officer Hacker. You are now conscripts of the Acheron Army. Failure to follow orders or comply with directives will result in your death. Do you understand?"

He was talking directly to me. He must have somehow sensed that I was their leader. I glanced back at Slik and Shen. Their eyes were wide, waiting for me to respond. I looked back to the ramrod straight Polit Officer.

"Yeah, we understand."

Hacker's face was square-jawed and closely shaven. A single laceration ran down his right cheek. The cut had been treated but was fresh, and it hadn't had time to scab yet.

"Outstanding," he replied with alarmingly good spirits. His black eyes contrasted with his fair skin and bright red hair. He turned to the nearest RUT and spoke. "Get them cleaned up and ready for transfer."

The trooper clicked his heels and came to attention. Hacker eyeballed Slik and Shen, shook his head dismissively, and turned away as he strode off. I felt that we had not seen the last of him.

***

As near as I could tell, we were in some kind of structure on the surface. I was not aware that the army had a surface installation. It made sense. They had to get into space from somewhere. Of course, we could be several levels down for all I knew. They guided us into an open central room and mixed in with other Toppers. There must have been about fifty of us from all over the surface. We were skinny, dirty, and scared.

They made us strip out of our clothes and then marched us through an automated shower facility that scrubbed off our filth, dried us, and then sprayed us with some kind of disinfectant. It smelled horrible, but truthfully, I'd never been cleaner. They shaved our heads nearly bald, unnervingly making us all look alike.

They gave us simple gray undergarments, and then we waited for what seemed like forever to get through a line for some kind of blood transfusion. The soldiers processing us said it was coboglobin, a synthetic blood that made us impervious to disease and infections. It turned our blood into an eerie amber and appeared clear under our skin.

Finally, we were led into another large room where we were fitted for our simple red uniforms with black belts and boots. I have always worn other people's clothes. I had never worn anything fitted for my body. As much as I wanted to hate it, it was not unpleasant.

We were filed into yet another room, this time a cafeteria with more food than any of us had ever seen in our entire lives. So, this is how the lower classes lived. We were given a stamped metal tray and simple metal utensils to eat. As the others gorged themselves, I sat and stared at the ear of perfect, yellow corn on my tray. I'd never seen such a beautiful piece of corn before. I picked it up with my hands to eat it and was slapped by a passing trooper. He yelled at me to use the utensils to hold the hot ear as I ate it. I only had a few minutes to eat, and then we were forced to turn in our trays and move to the next area. My stomach ached for more food as I swallowed my last bite.

***

The Acheron Army used rockets to get off the planet. They were a tried-and-true technology. I'd never heard of them taking off anywhere near where we lived, so we must have been far from our home turf. We boarded the rocket through a hatch on the side and moved to the rear of the narrow cabin area with seats on both sides of a narrow aisle. After taking my seat, I saw Slik sitting near me. I almost didn't recognize him with no hair. He nodded curtly to me, but I could tell he was still disgusted with being captured.

Given how clean I was, how nearly full my belly was, and how decent we'd been treated since being conscripted, my bitterness was slipping away. I was more concerned about our direction because I knew it couldn't be good.

Movement caught my eye a row ahead of me. It was Shen. Her hair had been shaved, too, but I recognized her dark, piercing eyes. The scabs on her face were nearly gone. Her elfin face wasn't as hard to look at anymore. She was no beauty, but she wasn't ugly anymore, either. She gave me a half smile and then turned around.

I didn't recognize anyone else around me. Just a bunch of malnourished, skinny kids about my age who all looked terrified at what might happen next. I stared at the back of the seat ahead of me and tried to remain calm. Someone who had made this trip before me had scribbled words across the back of the seat. *Goodbye, cruel world.*

The cabin held about fifty conscripts. After an hour of waiting for the right conditions, we were told to prepare for launch. The rocket lay on its side until the last few minutes of the countdown, when it was rotated upright. There weren't any windows, so I had no idea where we were, which was probably a good thing. The cabin lights were turned off, and just a few red lights lit the narrow gray cabin.

A quick and building noise below us was followed by a

jolt backward into our seats as the rocket pushed upward. The stress on my chest became immense as we climbed into the sky. I knew we were heading into the eternal storm clouds above the planet because lateral forces pushed us from side to side. My inner ear could detect the motion, but I could only imagine what was happening outside. The rocket lurched and shuddered as our speed increased. It seemed like an eternity, and a couple of times, I was convinced that the rocket's body would collapse from the stress of the launch.

Finally, we rotated, and our speed really increased as the ride smoothed out. We must have gotten through the cloud layer and broken into space—at least, that's what I imagined. I could still feel the thrust from the rocket engines, but soon, there was no shaking, and then everyone's arms started floating in front of us.

For the next hour or more, we floated in our seats. A few unlucky Toppers threw up. Prompting a trooper to float by with a vacuum that sucked all the chunks up. I could have done without seeing that. My stomach was tight, but I managed to keep what I had eaten down.

***

Our rocket eventually docked with something in orbit. I didn't know what until we were herded out of the narrow cabin and into a docking tunnel that had narrow, horizontal slit windows in it. I slowed down long enough to push my nose against the cold glass. I couldn't believe what my own eyes saw.

We were docked to a metallic ring that encircled the planet Acheron. Below us were the swirling gray and red clouds of our home world. Out beyond the ring was the inky black void of space. Another conscript pushed me along before the line stopped entirely. Others took long looks out the narrow window, too. Each one had to be pushed along, mouths agape in wonder. I couldn't understand how we could walk on this ring station, much less how anyone could have built such a massive structure.

I was still taking in what I had seen when we entered a spacious room and were forced into a single, massive formation. There was enough space between our rows to allow training instructors to run through our ranks, randomly barking insults and orders. I focused on the shaved back of another man's head as the instructors went on their rampage. The only thing I could do was wonder what new level of hell I had just entered.

A short man in a red uniform started screaming at me.

"Are you deaf? Get the hell out of my formation, Topper!"

I stepped out of the formation and realized I was the only one not in a row. More conscripts arrived, and I returned to a newly formed gaggle of bald people. This time, I was in the first row and at the far right of a new formation. Little did I know, I was now in a leadership position - first element leader. I quickly looked to my left and saw Slik and Shen were in my element. I turned back around, feeling slightly better at being in the same group as they were.

A woman with short white hair and a black uniform similar to ours, except with unit markings, stood before our formation. Her shoulders were hunched forward, and her eyes were deep-set and tired. She looked as if she were about to start something that she knew would be long and arduous. Her shoulders rolled back as she stiffened before speaking.

"My name is Alex, and I'll be your squad sergeant. We are Gamma Squad." Her voice was slightly raspy and projected a deeper tone than most women. I later came to know that tone was the military command voice.

"For the next six months, you will eat, shit, and sleep when I tell you to. You'll do what I tell you, how I tell you, or you'll get spaced. Is that clear?"

A few people responded weakly, which launched her into a rage. She started screaming at us and walking through the formation. I heard insults and curses that I'd never heard before. It was an education.

"You Toppers will only answer with - Yes, Sergeant, at the top of your ragged lungs. Is that understood?"

This time, most of us responded, "Yes, Sergeant!"

She circled in front of us and sighed. "I can't hear them?" she said, in a volume that was not loud enough for anyone not standing in the front row to hear. I felt her ink-black eyes focused on me when she spoke.

I sucked in the cool air of the station and screamed at the top of my lungs.

"Yes, Sergeant!"

She shook her head, and I felt her gaze still on me.

The rest of the squad took my cue, and we all repeated it, this time together.

"Yes, Sergeant!"

She moved to the right side of our formation and belted out commands to start marching. We didn't know what the commands meant. We started walking together to a cadence that Alex called out for us.

We moved through the station, changing into a central corridor where our pace picked up, and we were jogging in step to Alex's ragged voice. That's when it hit me just how big this place was. We ran for several minutes before slowing down and eventually coming to a halt before an area marked barracks.

Alex ordered us into the barracks by elements, which I learned were all the people to my immediate left in the formation. I was an element leader on the first day of our training. There were ten people in each element and five elements. The barracks room was just big enough for ten bunks on each side, with a double wide center aisle where we stood by element before our bunks. There were two elements to each section of the barracks, with what looked like sliding hatches between each section. The hatches were all open, and Alex strode down the center aisle, ensuring we lined up correctly.

Then, she came to the center area and gathered herself as we waited for her to say something. She walked purposefully up and down the center aisle, inspecting each one of us with a critical eye. Her voice was at normal volume now, almost casual.

"What a shabby lot of misfits you are. But that's okay. You're all lumps of clay that I will sculpt into the most feared killing machines the army has ever known. All you have to do is mind my orders and we'll get along just fine. Is that understood?"

"Yes, Sergeant!"

She pointed to me and then to the other squad leaders. "You people are the squad leaders. Everyone in your squad is your responsibility. If one of your members lags or can't keep up with the rest of us, it is your duty to help them. If you fail in that duty, you will be replaced. Understood?"

Only the squad leaders shouted this time, "Yes, Sergeant!"

Alex continued pacing before us, both hands locked behind her back. "Tomorrow, we will board the Ioudus transport ship to the front. It will take us roughly six months to make the trip. By the time we arrive, you will all be fully trained killing machines. Understood?"

"Yes, Sergeant!"

***

It took me quite a while to fall asleep that first night in the Ring. That's what they called where we were. Officially, it was known as Gateway Ring, but everyone shortened it to Ring. Alex allowed us to pass by a viewport after we had dinner so we could see the Ring. I didn't know there was such a thing as we could never see it from the surface. Nobody in our tribe had ever heard of anyone glimpsing the sky, much less what was high above it. The metallic structure extended around the planet's curve, fading as it dipped behind miles of atmosphere from Acheron. None of us had ever seen the stars, either. She had to tell us they were suns, but very far away. The sun was always a reddish ball of diffuse light for us, but it was incredibly bright and round from orbit. I couldn't even imagine how far away we'd have to be to see a star as just a pinpoint of light.

Alex said thousands of people lived on the Ring, and most were involved in building weapons for the war. I asked her how we could walk on the Ring, and she said it had to do with the spin of the Ring, forcing us outward and allowing us to feel as if we were on solid ground. It sounded like magic to me. My education consisted of my elders passing down what they had learned from their elders by word of mouth. We didn't have schools, only mentors.

I lay awake for hours, taking in all that had happened on

my first day in the Acheron Army. It wasn't all as bad as I had imagined it would be. At least not yet. We were clean, well-fed, and had a clear objective for the next six months. What happened after we got to the front kept me up. Alex said we were fighting humans from another planet around our sister star. She said they wanted to capture our world and kill us all so they could have its resources. That was why we fought. Hell, as Toppers, we never had resources, so right away, we couldn't care less about her war. But I didn't say that to her. I wasn't stupid.

***

Morning came with a blaring alarm and more yelling from Alex. How anyone could be that angry so early in the morning amused me. Our bunks had to be stripped, and the laundry piled into bins at the ends of the rooms. Then Alex showed us how to properly pack our duffel bags. We could store a week's worth of undergarments, three duty uniforms, and personal sanitary items we needed. I was amazed at how much we stuffed into those bags.

We were then marched to the cafeteria and allowed to eat long enough for me to finish my meal but not long enough for it to settle in my stomach. Alex marched us back to our barracks, where we picked up our duffel bags. We then marched single file by element down the main corridor of the Ring. We passed dozens of government workers who never acknowledged our existence.

Alex had me lead the squad into a terminal area with narrow observation windows looking out into deep space. We were not allowed to break formation, but she let us face the windows and catch our first glimpse of the ship that would be our home for the next six months. After a few minutes, Alex disappeared out of my sight.

The *Ioudas* wasn't a pretty ship. It was old and covered in chipped paint and blast marks from enemy weapons. There were streaks of yellow and gray all down its side as if they had run it through a cosmic mud puddle. Wherever it had been, it didn't look good at all.

Alex returned and shouted for us to head into the airlock passage that led to the ship. It was narrow and long and didn't have any windows. When I emerged into the Ioudas, the stale, dry air that circulated in the combat ship accosted my nose. Everything inside was the same flat gray color, accented only by chipped paint and grease stains. Alex led us deep into the bowels of the ship. All I could think of was how claustrophobic and cold it was.

The barracks on the *Ioudas* were not that different from those on the Ring—just older and more lived-in. We unpacked our bags and organized our things according to Alex's instructions. Nothing was ever going to be the way we wanted it anymore.

Afterward, she had us gather informally around her in the center aisle. She said we had a few minutes before we were to start training, and she wanted to answer our questions. Nobody spoke up, so I raised my hand. Alex pointed at me to speak.

"When are we coming back, Sergeant?"

Alex looked around at our squad and then spoke in a personable voice for perhaps the first time since we met her. "Most of you won't be coming back."

I looked around at everyone. I could see youthful enthusiasm in their eyes. They probably figured they would be the ones to come back. No matter what the odds. Not me. I was resigned to never coming back. It wasn't a hunch that I had or a morbid foreboding. I just figured there was nothing for me to come back for.

"If you do make it back, you will be given lower class status and a state job for life. But to be honest, the odds are against you."

I could hear the air letting out of everyone's hopes for a better life. I raised my hand again.

"How long will we be in the combat zone, Sergeant?"

"Good question. It will take us six months to make the journey to Betweos. We will be in the hot zone for the final two weeks of that journey. Enemy missiles can reach us at that point. You will be combat-dropped onto one of the moons until your mission is complete. When your mission ends, you will be ferried back to theIoudas until you are reassigned to another drop mission. This will continue for a year or until you're killed in action. If you survive that long, you will board either the *Ioudas* or one of the other transfer ships for a return trip."

Alex surveyed the deflated faces, and then her tone lifted. "Your best chance for making it home is to learn to fight. Learn your suit, your weapons, and your combat tactics. Help one another at all times. Teamwork saves lives and achieves the mission goals. Start to fracture as a group, and you will all die."

I saw the look in Slik's eyes as he smirked at me. He was a survivor like me. He might do alright. I saw Shen looking down at the floor with slumped shoulders. She was not a fighter like us. I didn't see her making it.

Alex came to attention. "Fall in!"

We all jumped up and headed for our bunks to stand at attention.

"Change into your PT uniform and be ready to move out in five."

Elpida

5

Our training was divided into three phases, imaginatively named for the colors of the Elysian Army - Yellow, Blue, and White. We'd all been through the Yellow Phase while still planetside. This basic military training taught you how to be a soldier. Now that we were in space and aboard our transfer ship, *Elpida*, they assigned us to our training squads and were technically in Phase Blue. Nobody knew what the White Phase was going to be about.

Phase Blue was all about team building, weapons training, and learning the combat rules. This is what I was there for, aside from killing the enemy. This was where I'd find out if I had what it took to be a great soldier. This is when I'd find out if I would honor my grandfather's memory or remain on the transfer ships like the other losers.

Early on, I had paired up with Saburo to be what the army called battle buddies. Every soldier was supposed to have a battle buddy for the duration of training and possibly beyond. In every exercise, we worked together so that by the end of training, we knew that person well enough to read them like a book. When Saburo jigged, I jagged, and together, we obliterated our enemies, each covering the other's butt.

Our military instructor for this phase was a tall, thin man with dark skin and white hair cut high and tight. His name was Sergeant Stickman, and he wore our gray duty uniform throughout the Blue Phase. His disk-shaped circular hat that every recruit associated with a military instructor was always tilted just so on his head. Stickman had earned the respect of everyone when he casually mentioned this was his second tour. He had fought with honor on at least two Betweos moons in battles while we were still in Yellow Phase. He was a combat veteran who knew how to fight and win. All of our Phase Two instructors were veterans, as we were part of the second wave of the current conjunction. Hector's wave would be the final if things went as planned by the command staff.

Stickman was quick to motivate us, but he could be patient when needed. Looking at his restful, dark eyes, I knew that he was a deep thinker. Nothing startled or surprised him. Stickman regarded everyone in his charge as individuals and treated us with respect. This was a far cry from my Yellow Phase instructor, Libreman, who enjoyed our pain and tried his best to flunk us out. It was his job to separate the soldiers from the civilians. To turn boys and girls into men and women worthy enough to wear the army uniform. It was only on graduation day that Libreman regarded us as something akin to humans. When he shook our hands and told us we were now soldiers, it meant the world to me and my fellow recruits. We had been initiated into the exclusive club of soldiering.

I knew that just doing what I was told in a timely manner would not win over Stickman, though. He expected everyone to have mastered the skills needed to follow orders. Stickman was more interested in whether you could work together as a proper combat team because following orders would not save our lives; only being vigilant and even creative would keep us alive.

A confidence course ran throughout *Elpida*, forcing us to work together to complete it. Every time we ran the course, it was different. Sometimes, there were physical challenges that no single soldier could overcome, and sometimes, there were puzzles that required two or more of us to complete. I enjoyed my time on the course. I was good at assessing new situations and devising a working strategy to overcome whatever problem faced me or my squad.

"You need to balance the rail upward until you can extend it across the pit," I coaxed Saburo.

The pit was two meters below us and filled with simulated lava. They adjusted gravity lower to simulate the first moon that we would fight on, Betwi-One. We all wore gray fatigue uniforms, not the combat suits we would eventually fight in. Our safety helmets had a visor screen that displayed tactical data in real time, not unlike the kind our combat suits would have.

Stickman stood off to the side, holographic lava flowing around him harmlessly. Two other soldiers were in the pit to catch us if we fell from the narrow beam we were perched on.

"I can't hold it up. It's too heavy," Saburo replied.

I could only see the static-filled image from Saburo's helmet camera. He was positioned behind a wall on the other side of me. "Sab, hold on to it and pan your head around the room. I must have missed something."

Saburo secured the beam and did as instructed. I stared at the tiny images on my visor. There was a post, just big enough for the rail in Saburo's hands. He was supposed to rest the beam on the post, and then we could traverse the beam to cross the lava pit. It was pretty simple, which is what I was afraid of. Nothing on Stickman's course was as simple as it seemed. There were usually more variables for a problem than first met the eye.

Finally, I realized what we should do. "Okay, look at the simulated gravity," I told Saburo.

"One-third normal."

"Right, so if you use the rail as a pole and vault yourself to the side, the lower gravity will work to your advantage. Then you can toss it back to me, and I'll do the same."

I watched Saburo's camera look around and then down at the beam. My big friend was working out the math in his head. Finally, he mumbled over the comm, "Okay, I think we can do that."

"You got this, Corporal!"

"Time's a-wastin', soldiers," Stickman's voice echoed in our ears.

Saburo got to his feet and hoisted the rail over his broad shoulder. After a few quick breaths, he ran the short length of the beam he was on and used the rail he was carrying to vault over the lava bed to safety. He got to his feet and scrambled to face the opening where I was crawling out onto the foot beam. Saburo's arms were up in victory.

"Nicely done," I commended him. His goofy smile was ear to ear.

I looked at Stickman, who took the vault rail away from Saburo and shortened it by a third. It retracted inside itself to shorten. "Lava's a bitch, man."

Saburo held up the now much shorter rail, and I bit my lower lip. Crap. Now it's too short. I didn't account for that. I motioned for my battle buddy to toss it to me anyway. Stickman watched us with interest, choosing to remain silent.

"There's no way you'll make it now," Saburo shouted.

I looked over at Stickman, whose dark face was implacable. I hefted the beam and walked backward to the start of my foot beam, giving myself all the running room before jumping. I knew I wouldn't jump with or without the rail for a pole if we were at full gravity. But I wasn't in my home world anymore, and this was not an impossible leap on Betwi-One.

I tossed the shortened rail into the fake lava and ran along the beam until I reached the end, where I leaped as high as possible. I easily landed in the safe area beside Saburo, who helped me and shook his head. "I'm glad your scrawny butt came after me!"

I smiled. "Me too."

Stickman was already directing the helpers to reset the course. He wouldn't praise anyone unless they did something unusual to pass the test. So I guess that was what he was looking for us to do all along. Later that day, Saburo came to me during our time. His voice was low so that nobody could overhear him.

He looked around and then back at me. "Remember that exercise today with the lava pit?"

I nodded.

"I did some asking around. We were the only ones to

pass it."

He lifted a dark eyebrow and grinned at me. Then he made a fist and pumped it as a sign of victory for our two-man team. As he walked back to his bunk, I looked around at the others and wondered why none of them had been able to consider the lower gravity. It seemed obvious to me.

We had a few minutes before lights out, and I checked my dispatches. I flipped through the messages from home, reading some from my dad and one from Hector. My father had taken the brunt of my mother's anger that I had escaped their clutches and was now heading into harm's way. For what it was worth, though, he did admit that he was proud of me. I didn't respond to them because I wanted to keep my head in the right space for my training. They both knew this and didn't expect my replies until we reached Betweos.

There were a bunch of messages from Trille, but I couldn't bring myself to read them. I'm not sure exactly why. We were engaged to be married, and millions of kilometers separated us. I was too scared to be seen blubbering into my pillow when I read them. I promised myself that I would catch up on them when the training was over and respond.

***

The *Elpida* was a long, spindly ship with a rotating ring section that allowed for gravity and a massive nuclear pulse fusion drive that pushed it across the void between the twin stars of the system. Forward of the rotating ring were the drop tubes and the weapons array for self-defense against incoming Arachian missiles. It was originally a glossy white color, but several trips to Betweos had left it flat gray with rust streaks from the sulfur volcanoes of Betwi-One.

Life aboard the starship was highly disciplined and, at times, claustrophobic. It always seemed to smell like sweaty troops and seared steak. A crewman I met in my first week aboard said the burnt smell was what space itself smelled like. I didn't really believe him until we reached Betweos and I actually climbed into the launch tubes for my first combat drop. The entire room where they suited us up and inserted us into the tubes reeked of hot metal and welding fumes. Once ensconced inside my combat armor, all I could smell was plastic and my own funk.

The barracks were tight, and the bunks narrow, with thin mattresses in plastic-sculpted beds. Everything was the same flat gray color, even the mattress pads and sheets. The bathrooms were unisex with no privacy and Spartan fixtures. It was not a warm and inviting place, but it was our home for nearly six months.

Sometimes, I would lay in my bunk and listen for the fusion drive to fire, giving the whole ship a slight nudge forward. Day by day, week by week, we got closer to the giant silver planet that was Betweos. I remember my grandfather describing the cloud storms of Betweos as the most beautiful and terrifying thing he had ever witnessed. He recalled looking up at Betweos from the surface of one of the moons and getting the unmistakable feeling that he was about to fall upward into the sky. The power and majesty of the planet would pull him into a long, slow plunge into its massive clouds. I yearned to see that for myself.

Our training soon began to focus more on weapon familiarization. The Elysian Army called it Constant Carry. It entailed being assigned a weapon that was never allowed to be out of your sight. Whenever you were caught without it, you were punished. Usually, with extra physical conditioning and cleaning, the nastiest parts of the ship. I know because I once went to the shower without my weapon. After that, I shit, showered and slept with the damn thing. My rifle and I were the same.

Some soldiers named their rifles, but it was not a requirement. You were expected to not just carry it constantly but maintain it and be as familiar with it as you were with your own body. We memorized its serial number and practiced taking it apart, cleaning it, and putting it back together a million times.

Stickman was a stickler for details. He knew every weapon better than any recruit could hope to know their own rifle. If you let your rifle get dirty or show excessive wear, he would notice it and ride your butt until you repaired or cleaned it to his high standards. Nobody was immune from his intense scrutiny. Not even me.

"Soldier!" Stickman shouted from across the room.

Everyone's head spun around to face the instructor, except for one. Mine. I was too focused on my weapon. The cold, flat, multi-chamber barrel was smooth as I ran my fingers along its bare metal. I was sitting in my bunk, putting the weapon back together while wearing a blindfold. I couldn't see the instructor and thus didn't know I was in the man's sight.

Stickman strode across the room, heavy feet falling hard on the grated metal floor until he stood over me. I looked up and cocked my head. I could sense his presence.

"Your weapon, soldier. Hand it to me."

I jumped up, came to attention with the rifle at my side. Then I offered the weapon to him with a proper present arms hoist. Stickman took the rifle and immediately checked the charging block for dirt. Finding none, he inspected the weapon from barrel to stock in a series of crisp movements that recalled a precision drill team member. I stood at attention, listening to the crack and patting while waiting for my weapon.

Stickman returned it to me, and I secured it to my side. I could hear the sound of a knife being unsheathed, and then I felt the blade against my temple. A quick pull cut the cloth blindfold, and it fell from around my eyes. I focused ahead as Stickman stuck his face uncomfortably close to mine.

"Your weapon is wet. Too much oil can attract dust and dirt."

"Yes, Sergeant!"

Stickman pulled away slowly and then left the room. I sighed in relief as Saburo rushed up to me.

"Are you alright?"

I nodded, picked up the blindfold, and shoved it into the nearest garbage chute. I couldn't use it anymore, and getting a new one was not easy. I wondered if Stickman was trying to tell me not to waste my time with it anymore.

"It's okay. I deserved that."

Saburo shook his head. "I thought he was going to cut you, man."

I shrugged. "Nah, he likes me too much. Can't you tell?"

Saburo did a double take. "Could have fooled me."

I started slowly taking my weapon apart again while wiping it down. Sure enough, it was a bit oily. Stickman was hard, but he was fair, and over time, I began to respect the man more and more.

***

One time in primary school, I was called out for pencil fighting. I was straight-up guilty. My buddy and I had reinforced our wooden pencils with metal rods. From the back of my biology class, you could hear us thumping our "pencils" together, trying to break each other's metal rod. But we couldn't. All the teacher heard was the ting of metal on metal. That walk from my classroom to the principal's office was the longest walk of my life until today.

When my name suddenly blared out of the ship's PA system, calling me to the Political Officer's room, my heart sank, and I felt tremendous guilt, just like that day when my teacher sent me to the principal's office. Only this time, I hadn't done anything wrong. At least not knowingly. My mind raced through the events of the past several days, searching for what I could have possibly done to have pissed off Lacithe. I was fixing my gig line and rubbing the tops of my polished boots on my legs as I wound my way to the PO's Office.

One hard knock was how they taught us to report. My knuckles rapped against the airlock door, barely making a sound. Should I knock again, harder, or should I wait and see what happens? I decided to wait. After what seemed like forever, the hatch slid open, and I could see Lacithe sitting behind an imposing metal desk. My knees almost gave out on me as I stepped inside.

The door slid shut with a sudden jolt that caused me to cringe. Lacithe was the most influential person in our chain of command. He could send us back to Elysia or ensure that we graduated into combat missions. You didn't piss off the man, and you tried to never, ever get called before him. For anything.

I stayed at attention, staring firmly at the wall over the man's head, and snapped a crisp salute.

"Corporal Jered, reporting as ordered, sir."

Lacithe sat back in his chair and looked me up and down slowly. He undoubtedly noticed my sweaty palms and the slight shudder in my legs. It's a good thing he couldn't hear my racing heart. I wished that I couldn't feel it. He waved a half salute, and I lowered my arm smartly.

"Do you know why I've asked to see you today, Corporal?"

I resisted the urge to nod and belted, "Sir, no, sir!"

"You can stand at ease," Lacithe said in a conversational tone.

I don't know what was worse: the relaxed tone of his voice or the fact that I could look him in the eye while at ease. I kept my eyes forward but relaxed my stance.

"You're here today because your squad instructor thinks you should be promoted. He wants you to be a Squad Sergeant. Do you know what that means, Corporal?"

I thought about it. It meant that I would be a non-commissioned officer – a good thing. It also meant that I would be responsible for all fifty squad members, not just the ten members of my element. I was moved into the element leader role on my first day. I figured it was just the luck of the draw, but now I realize that even back then, Stickman had his eye on me.

I had never heard of anyone making sergeant while still in Phase Blue. Hell, I didn't think anyone made sergeant until after their first drop. But I was still pretty green and didn't realize that someone had to lead the squad into combat, and it wouldn't be the training instructors. This meant someone had to be selected into a squad leadership role before we dropped.

"Sir, I'll be responsible for my entire squad."

I could tell he approved my answer because I could see him in my peripheral vision. For whatever reason, I decided to look down at him at that point. He was still staring coldly at me with his deep-set eyes. His light blue, spiked hair was the same color as his uniform.

"Correct. Do you have what it takes to lead people into combat?"

I did not expect him to ask that. But I didn't even

consider it for a moment.

"Sir, yes, sir!"

Lacithe gave me a side eye and then looked down at his monitors. "You're the son of Joros, grandson of Jarna. Your grandfather was a great warrior for the Elysian people. But your father was a dud. Never did a combat drop for his entire tour. Do you expect me to believe that military talent in your family skips a generation?"

I didn't know how to answer that. I wanted to defend my father's service and blame my grandfather for his lack of combat experience, but that would have made Jarna seem weak in this man's eyes.

"Sir, yes, sir."

Lacithe glanced up at me momentarily and then back to his screens. "Farmer's son from the lowlands. Moderate education and did well in primary training but didn't make the honor squad—only one visit to the infirmary. I don't know, son. I'm not seeing anything special about you."

He sat back in his chair and crossed his arms. "Do you care to defend yourself?"

I sensed a trap, so I kept my trap closed. He waited for a nervously long moment and then referenced his screens again.

"Your squad instructor said that you're the only soldier to complete the last challenge of his confidence course. He also claims to have caught you field stripping and cleaning your rifle blindfolded. Is that true, Corporal?"

"Sir, yes, sir."

Lacithe pushed himself to his feet, his eyes on mine as he rose a few inches over me. "Stickman also said you could be trouble. Do you know why he would warn me about that?"

Crap, I had no idea. I paused and then uttered, "Sir, no, sir."

Lacithe leaned across the now tiny table between us until his black eyes aligned with mine.

"Because leaders can influence people, for better or worse. Do I make myself clear, Sergeant Jered?"

I swallowed hard.

"Sir, yes, sir!"

He backed away from me and sat down. His attention was already focused on his screens.

"I'll be watching you, Sergeant. Dismissed."

I came to attention, saluted, and then did an about-face. The blast door slid open, and I took off down the narrow corridor back to my barracks.

Elpida

6

Phase White came sooner than anyone thought it would. One day, we were slogging through a nasty obstacle course, and the next, we were sitting in a cramped classroom like a bunch of kids who suddenly realized summer was over. But this wasn't like secondary school. It was better. We would be learning tactics and formations, both our own and the enemy's. Despite the annoying body aches and pains from training, I sat upright in my hard metal chair, ready to learn.

Not everyone was as enthusiastic as me. I noticed a few people grateful to just be sitting. I wondered how long they would go before succumbing to sleep. Beside me was the girl with silver hair. I was close enough to read her name tape: Selina. Nice enough name. Her hair was pulled back from her face, and I could see her eyes were as ash-neutral as her hair. There was an awareness in her glance that most others didn't have. She was not your average soldier. I thought she was merely going through the motions in training. Almost as if she had no intentions of actually fighting once we got into combat. That troubled me. I knew I had seen her face in the Peacer crowd, and she was not wearing the Elysian uniform. She had been wearing an overcoat. Thinking back on it now seems strange, considering we left in late summer. Maybe she was hiding her uniform with the coat. Maybe she didn't want to draw the attention that Saburo and I did. That would have been smart.

Stickman came into the room and lectured about what to expect in Phase White. There was less yelling, even more attention to detail, and more emphasis on why we did what we did. It all sounded good to me. When class was dismissed, Sergeant Stickman called me into his office. After what happened with Lacithe, I was more than a little apprehensive.

I stood before the thin metal door of the Instructor's billet. They slept in private quarters just off our main barracks. They had their bunks, storage space, and a tiny desk. I knew that because I had to clean their billets regularly. Stickman's billet was empty of any reminders from home. There was only a surreal picture of Betweos's gaseous storms. I thought the picture was enigmatic. Was there something about Stickman that was stormy or unsettled? Or did he just think it was beautiful?

My palms were sweaty despite my knowing that I wasn't in any kind of trouble. I rapped once on the thin metal door. It opened immediately, taking me by surprise. Inside, Stickman was sitting cross-legged on a padded mat. He was wearing exercise tights and appeared to be in deep meditation. His eyes were closed, his hands open, and he rested on his knees. A single wavering light on his shelf reminded me of a candle. The main room lights were dim.

I stepped inside, and the door slid shut behind me.

Stickman opened his eyes and motioned for me to sit with him on the floor. I sat across from him, my legs also crossed.

"What do you think of the White Phase of your training, Sergeant Jered?"

I wasn't used to being called sergeant yet. It still felt odd, especially when Stickman addressed me with it.

"More interesting. I like it."

Stickman studied me for a moment with his coal-black eyes.

"A warrior must be able to calm himself when all those around him are panicking. To learn this, you must practice meditation."

Stickman closed his eyes and took a deep breath through his nostrils, letting it out through his mouth. Then he opened his eyes again and told me to breathe the same way. I closed my eyes and breathed in through my nose and out again through my mouth.

"A warrior's mind is his first, best weapon," Stickman intoned.

"So the smarter I am, the more deadly I will be?" I asked.

Stickman mumbled something I couldn't decipher. "Something like that. We each fight to the best of our physical abilities. Some of us are stronger, and some are quicker, but all of us must be smarter than the enemy."

I smirked. "That's a pretty low bar, right? I mean, how smart are hive minds?"

Stickman didn't respond. I opened my eyes to see him looking at me.

"Smarter than you might think. The point is that you must always be thinking faster and smarter than they are. Study your combat tactics and know your platoon's abilities. But to get the upper hand, you must also know the enemy's tactics and abilities."

I processed that for a moment. "How do I learn their tactics and abilities?"

Stickman raised a long pointer finger. "Patience, son. I can only teach you what you are willing to accept."

"I'm willing."

His face relaxed into a toothy grin.

***

Classroom work continued, but now we learned more about our enemy. How they fought, and what their capabilities were. I soaked it in, eager to prove my willingness to learn. Weapons specialists taught some of our classes and some by tacticians, but the ones I most looked forward to were the ones taught by Stickman. His classes were usually about either squad tactics or enemy tactics. My favorite was called entos military doctrine. He introduced us to novel concepts like Distributed Command and Control and Swarming.

"Entos Command and Control is not limited to one central location. They use a distributed method that creates combat cells capable of moving rapidly and attacking our defenses multiple times and from multiple directions simultaneously. Their interlinked suits with multiple scanners and sensors make this possible. Some believe the insect mind is perfectly suited to allow them to form smaller groups and for leader bugs to control each combat cell."

I raised my hand and Stickman pointed to me as he walked around the classroom.

"Is this related to the Hive Mentality I've heard mentioned before?"

Stickman bobbed his head and responded so everyone could hear him clearly above the constant bass pulse of the starship's drive. "Yes, and no. Swarming is a well-known military tactic that humans have used throughout our history. It's only been since the Bug War that we've seen the most sophisticated version of it. The degree of integration in the Acheron Army is the only thing that has kept this war going for as long as it has.

"The Elysian Army has always been and will always be the larger combatant in this war. Despite the fact that their evolutionary cousins number in the billions, sentient bugs have greater resource needs than even a single human. Meaning that it takes their world far more natural resources to raise enough soldiers to threaten Elysia."

Another soldier raised her hand. It was Selina. "Could it simply be that the Acheron Army has used up all its resources and, therefore, has to find other ways to combat our superior numbers?"

Stickman grinned. I could tell he was enjoying this intellectual exercise. "Yes, that might very well be the case. But in the end, I don't care what reasons they have for fighting an asymmetrical war. I only care about how I can defeat them. And so should all of you."

Stickman circled back around to the front of the classroom. "Regular soldier bugs only communicate with the cell leaders. So, if you can take out the cell leader, they will continue to execute their last known attack order. It's your job to find these cell leaders and take them out as quickly as possible. Then it's just mowing down the remaining enemy soldiers."

I glanced at Selina, who had a disgusted look on her face for some reason.

"Easy, right?" Stickman shrugged.

We all knew that nothing about soldiering was easy. There was always a catch, and we remained silent, waiting for our instructor to drop the other shoe. Stickman didn't disappoint.

"Identifying a swarm leader is next to impossible. They are not marked in any special way, and they have no special equipment to differentiate them from regular soldiers."

So how do we find them, Sarge?" Saburo asked.

"You have to be smarter than them. You have to be able to assess what the attack is after and recognize common movements and attack vectors that the enemy uses. And that is what this class is all about. Teaching you lugs how the enemy fights so you can alter your tactics and defeat them without waiting for Combat Control to tell you what's happening and how to move."

I slowly shook my head and bit my lower lip. This was the good stuff.

***

Several weapons were placed on a table in the armory room. They didn't look familiar to any of us, and many whispers were deducing that they were, in fact, enemy weapons. I was closest to one of the smaller rifles that looked similar to what we were now all carrying everywhere we went. It was larger than our rifles but looked like it was built on a different scale than a human.

"Sergeant, are these grips designed for entos hands, or can a human use them too?" I asked Stickman.

He picked up the rifle and placed his large, dark hand across the grip. He could barely wrap his fingers around the circumference.

"The entos use these weapons in their armored suits. Actual bug hands are no bigger than our own."

Everyone seemed to agree that it made sense. Stickman hit a switch on the back side of the rifle, and it resized itself in his arms to something with a smaller grip. The rest of the weapons remained oversized. Mouths fell open as we gasped in disbelief. What kind of crazy engineering was this?

"If the entos are not wearing their armor, their trusty Zed dash Niner can be resized to fit their four-fingered digits."

He flipped the massive rifle over to show us the switch.

"Adaptive rifles are just the beginning, folks. The entos technology has always been a generation ahead of anything our people have come up with. The fact that we can even stick with them in a fight always amazed the hell out of me."

Stickman handed me the rifle. It was so heavy I could barely hold it up. He motioned for me to set it down on the table and I complied with the assistance of Saburo. We examined the rifle closer. I flipped the switch, and we watched closer as the rifle morphed just enough to make it unmanageable to a single human. I ran my finger along the barrel and felt its texture and the cold of the metal. It wasn't all metal, though. Some parts were a composite material, and others felt more plastic.

When the rifle was in the smaller grip mode, I could see three circles along the barrel and wondered what they meant in bug language. Saburo stood back after a minute, and we both let the others get closer to examine it. He and I moved on to the next weapon, which was just about twice the size of the first one.

Stickman tapped the barrel of the massive weapon. "This is their SAW, Squad Automatic Weapon. She's a beast, isn't she?"

Saburo and I nodded in complete awe of its potential firepower. Why the hell didn't we have something this badass?

"This is the B Dash Fiver. Almost as much firepower as a tank and capable of sustained fire rates nearly double that of our own SAW."

Eyes grew as big as the weapon.

"How the hell do we defend against that thing?" Saburo asked.

"Keep your head down," Stickman suggested.

I slapped my arm around Saburo and laughed at his stunned reaction. He eventually lightened up. Stickman moved on with the demonstration, including a few enemy pistols and a disrupter rifle. The disrupter didn't fire a plasma or explosive round. It knocked out EMP or Electromagnetic Pulse bursts that could disable Elysian weapons and, more critically, our suits of armor.

"This relatively innocuous rifle can ruin your day faster than anything else on the table. Fortunately for us, they are still rare on the battlefield. But if you encounter them, make taking them out your top priority, or you'll be dead before you can do anything about it."

Saburo gave me a raised eyebrow when he noticed the sober look on my face. We both focused on fixing the weapon in our memories.

Stickman stepped away from the table of enemy weapons and directed everyone's attention to the screen behind him. It displayed NO QUARTER in bold white letters on a black background.

"Under no conditions are you allowed to ever, and I mean ever, take a bug soldier as your prisoner. If you find yourself in single combat with one, you will do everything in your power to kill it, and if you can't, you are to leave the area immediately. Never follow a bug anywhere. Never try to render a wounded bug medical assistance."

Nobody had any issue with those rules, but Stickman took a moment to elaborate.

"First, they are not built like you and me. They are insects. Sure, they are tall like us and move similarly to us, but they are every bit as alien to us as a cockroach. Do not harbor any sympathy for the enemy. If you do, you will be killed or worse."

Selina raised her hand, and Stickman pointed to her. "Do they have a similar policy towards us?"

"No. They will take prisoners every chance they get."

Everyone looked around at each other with curiosity. Stickman's volume was lower than before, and we could all tell he was earnest with us. Several of us leaned in to hear what he said next.

"Nobody's ever returned after being captured by the Arachian Army. Some have speculated that prisoners are shipped back to their home world and used as slave laborers. Others believe prisoners are cooked and eaten."

Some disgusted faces looked around nervously after that, including mine. Stickman paused for effect and said, "Most experts now agree that prisoners are kept alive and made into hosts for entos larvae."

One soldier grabbed his mouth and turned away. He gulped hard but didn't lose it. Sweat broke out across my forehead, and I wiped it with my sleeve. Suddenly, it was hot in the armory. The thought of being violated in such a way was nauseating for everyone in the room.

"Don't be captured, and don't show any mercy to the monsters."

Ioudas

7

B asic military training started with four weeks of grueling exercise and boring classes about military customs, courtesies, and drilling. Nobody liked it, and everyone eventually learned to keep their traps shut about how much they hated it. Days would start with a five-kilometer run around the perimeter of the rotating ring, followed by a sparse meal and then four hours of lecture followed by several hours of drill that found us back in our billets for another hour of instruction on how to fold our damn clothes and make our damn beds.

Our instructor, Alex, would hammer anyone not performing to their usual ability in anything she was teaching us, from creasing our underwear to advanced drill moves. Slackers found themselves doing extra details, like cleaning the toilets or scrubbing the floors. I soon learned that even if I kept my nose clean and performed to expectations, I still did my fair share of crap details.

After the tenth straight day of folding, refolding, and creasing our red dress uniforms until they measured up to Alex's metal ruler, she finally told us why she was so damn focused on minutia. "It's the little things that get you killed in combat. If we can't trust you to make your bed and fold your clothes properly, how can we trust you with an expensive combat suit?"

I figured she had a point. But I knew some Toppers who couldn't find their way home from a patrol, no matter how many times they covered the same landscape of pipes and conduits. Somehow, though, they could take down two RUTs with fewer shots than I could, which made them just as valuable to me.

Slik had issues doing bodyweight exercises, and his lifting was pathetic. The guy was scrawny as a ruler and just about as thin. The one thing he could do better than everyone else was run. His lean muscles pumped his legs faster than pistons. Alex would get on his case pretty bad, though, for being unable to deadlift his body weight. She told him he was destined to be a scout and would probably be the first in the squad to die because scouts had a shorter lifespan in combat due to their lighter armor and smaller size. Telling him he would die quicker didn't seem to motivate him noticeably. I knew that argument wouldn't work with Slik. She would have been better off telling him he could kill more of the enemy if he bulked enough to wear the main battle suits. After I mentioned this to Slik, the kid started keeping on his muscles, and by the end of BMT, he could lift the minimum amount to be with us in the regulars.

I had no trouble keeping up with Alex and the other squad mates. I hated running but fought the pain like everyone else, including Shen. Her scabs treatment and regular diet began filling her out and toning her muscles. She was looking pretty damn good to just about everyone. Shen seemed to enjoy the attention, something she had never experienced until now. I sometimes stared at her and had to look away to keep my thoughts clear.

Sex with the other trainees was forbidden until we had graduated. Cameras in the barracks and the open shower and toilet facilities made getting away with it just about impossible. That didn't stop people from getting off. It just made it harder not to watch.

***

Graduation day was like every other day, except we were all ordered into what they called the Indoctrination Room. Just the name of it set us on edge. The uniform was dress reds, crisply creased shirts and pants with shiny black belts and boots. I hated the Acheron dress uniform almost as much as the military. It was stiff and uncomfortable and restricted my movements, making me feel like a puppet trooper.

The room was cold and empty, with black walls and bare metal floors. The only light came from a narrow spot that glared down on us like a back-room confessional. Polit Officer Hacker entered the room wearing a blue and white uniform that nobody had seen before. It was bright and impressive in its military cut and polish. I wondered if this was what we would wear after BMT. Alex ordered us into open ranks and then put us at ease. The harsh spotlight followed Hacker around the room as he weaved in and out of our formation.

"I want you people to take a long, hard look at my uniform. This is the uniform of your enemy, the Elysian Army. From now on, I am your enemy. I will do everything I can to make you hate me and everything I represent. Do you understand?"

Too late. I already hated his ass from the moment I first laid eyes on him, I thought to myself.

The squad came to attention and answered as one, "Sir, yes, sir!"

Hacker made his way to the front of the squad and faced us with a look of utter disgust on his scared, pale face. "Acheron Toppers are the lowest form of life. You're genetically inferior to us Elysians. We consider you lower than the lowest, diseased rats that feed on our garbage. In fact, to us, you're all considered vermin. Something to be eradicated from our system, like pests. The sooner you're all gone, the better off the system will be. The safer it will be for the rightful heirs of Elysia."

What the hell was he even talking about? His words didn't have much of an effect on any of us. We had never known a threat from Elysia. Living in abject poverty and evading capture by the Acheron Army was more of a concern than some faraway world we had never seen or heard much about. The war was only important to the lower classes.

Hacker seemed to know we'd be apathetic to him and his war. He stopped before Slik and stared into his dark eyes. Slik's mouth half formed a smirk in return. I thought for sure

Hacker would take his head off for it.

"We killed everyone you left behind on the surface. One of our attack drones murdered all of your family, friends, and gang mates," Hacker said. Slik's smirk faded as his face went hard. Hacker moved on.

I whispered so that only Slik could hear me. "No, he didn't. It's an act."

Hacker stood in front of Shen. Her eyes struggled to stay focused past the intimidating Polit Officer.

"We killed your grandmother. One of our incendiary rounds burned her to a crisp. Your little sister? Killed by residual explosions from the drone strikes. What was your tribe sister's name? Crys? The automatic guns quartered her."

Shen shook out of anger and fear. Hacker moved away towards the next man as Shen's tears flowed down her cheeks. She resisted wiping them for fear of reprisal.

"We killed your father. His name was Krenn, wasn't it?"

The man nodded. "He couldn't outrun the drones, either. They cut him in half. It was a mess."

The man didn't react, so Hacker moved on. He stood in front of me next. I drew a breath, anticipating the worst.

"You were the leader of your gang, weren't you? Not much of a gang, was it? Our drones killed every member of your group that the Acheron Army left behind. A dozen more roaches killed right in their shit pile."

I didn't react. Because I knew better. I had seen his troops tossing Grim's body and the others into a pile. This was all an act to get us to hate our enemy. Hacker sensed my disbelief. He pushed closer, breaking into my personal space. His stern face cracked a sinister grin. His voice was a whisper. "One of your hoodlum friends got a shot off at me," he pointed to the scar on his cheek. "He was a rabid little one called Grim."

I looked directly into his soulless black eyes.

"Oh, are you perhaps wondering what happened to little Grim? Our drones took him out. He's quite dead now."

I didn't blink. "I don't believe you."

Hacker's twisted smile remained as he turned to the blank wall before the squad and raised his arms. The walls materialized into a holographic view of the surface of Acheron. We all recognized the landscape immediately. It was our home turf. It was so real. I felt as if I were back on Acheron.

The bleak surface was even more so with fires burning from huge blast craters. Columns of thick, black smoke trailed into the dark skies. Bodies were strewn about in various contorted death poses. The recording moved over the corpses, lingering so that the dead could be recognized. Acheron Army RUTs were bent over them, trying to help those clinging to life. A crashed drone with blue roundels was the only hint of who had attacked.

Some members of the squad fell to their knees, crying in anguish as they recognized family members. Shen was one of them after seeing her tribal sister's body torn to pieces. Hacker turned around with a disgustingly gleeful look on his face. "We did this to your friends and family. We killed every one of them! It was the first drone attack of its kind on your home world. Your planetary defenses never saw it coming and could not protect the surface from direct attack by our war drones. It was a glorious success and marked a turning point in the war with Acheron. It's only a matter of time now before we destroy your army at Betweos and cut loose our interplanetary war drones to permanently exterminate all life on Acheron."

I no longer had any hope that anyone had survived the massacre, but I didn't for one moment believe it was the enemy who had killed them. I was convinced Hacker had slaughtered the Toppers and made it look like an enemy attack. Ultimately, it didn't matter if he was telling the truth about the attack. From now on, Hacker was going to pay for what had happened. I would focus all of my ire on just one target, not Elysia. Somehow, in some way, I would kill Hacker or die trying.

***

The secondary battle arms were attached to Alex's waist and controlled by her mind as if they were artificial limbs. They traveled smoothly around her waist on fluid tracks, letting her face two opponents simultaneously. Her armor was painted a bright, safety orange and was half the thickness and weight of the actual battle armor.

Two squad members were sparring with her, Slik in front and Evid behind her, as she demonstrated proper fighting form. "The waist-mounted SBAs or Secondary Battle Arms are designed to protect your ass when your attention is elsewhere during trench fighting. Once activated, they are guided by sensors on your armor and work completely independently."

She twisted and moved around the training room, her SBAs wielding a rifle while she held a plasma cutter in her arms. Her movements were fluid and seemed second nature to her. The movements of my squad mates seemed slow and lethargic by comparison.

"Okay, Evid, you attack me from behind, and Slik here will take me face on. Observe how the SBA's let me ignore Evid's attack."

Alex motioned for both of them to attack her. Evid lunged towards her, and the SBAs engaged him in basic sparring moves. He could barely press his attack, spending all his energy on defensive moves. Meanwhile, Slik's attack was more aggressive, with full swings of his rubber beam cutter. Alex was easily able to defend herself without looking behind her.

Evid backed away and tried an alternative approach. One of Alex's SBAs grabbed his arm and pinned him down while the second mechanical arm brought the cutter across his chest in a simulated kill. Slik's attack was thwarted by a nasty jab that ended up with his neck locked in her elbow and her cutter across his throat. She had killed them both in seconds and earned a new level of respect from all the other troopers, including me.

Alex let them go and turned around to face Evid as he got up. "In an actual battle, you would have been dispatched by my Personal Defense Cannons without me knowing you were there."

Avid shook his head as both men returned to the ranks. Alex resumed the combat-ready position. I noticed someone staring at me and saw Shen lifting a challenging eyebrow.

***

Shen's attack pressed through my cutter, forcing her helmet into my grill. Her war scream scrunched her face as she blasted me with her rifle. I felt her warm breath across my sweaty face. We were both wearing the SBAs, but her arms wrapped around my chest and squeezed my breath out of me. I grimaced, waiting for Alex to call mercy, but she only praised Shen's brutal attack.

Fine. I tried to twist out of the hold but could not free myself with brute force. My SBAs adjusted beneath me, and suddenly, she flew off of me and hit hard on the padded mat.

"Gaven, you better wake up, or she will get you!" Alex shouted. She blew her whistle. Shen had flipped herself over and was pressing her attack again without pause.

She twisted through my defensive posture as I struggled against my SBAs, fighting them instead of letting them help me. She took advantage of this and quickly pinned me down against the mat. Her sweaty hair dripped onto my face as she grimaced above me.

"What's the matter? Am I slowing you down?" she taunted.

I shook off the sweat and craned my head up to her face to kiss her firmly. The move startled her and allowed me a moment to adjust my mechanical arms to gain enough leverage to toss her off of me. In the blink of an eye, I was on top of her, pinning her firmly to the mat.

"Not yet," I replied.

The move impressed the other squad members. They applauded my efforts and whistled their approval. Shen stared incredulously at me as Alex blew her whistle, and I got off her.

"Very original, Gaven. But kissing the enemy is hard when you're both in armor."

I shrugged and gave Shen a playful smile. Her hardened look soured my enthusiasm.

"Okay, people, let's de-suit and return the SBAs to the armorer. Hit the showers before the mess call."

As everyone started helping each other out of the SBAs, Slik edged closer to me to whisper, "She's pretty sweet, huh?"

I frowned, remembering the saltiness of her sweat. "More like bitter."

My response confused Slik, but he didn't risk pressing the matter as we stored our practice armor.

***

Steam filled the shower stalls as recruits hurriedly soaped up and rinsed off to make room for the next squad. There were only enough sprayer heads for ten troopers, and they only had water for two minutes. We lathered and rinsed. Then, the air dryers buffeted us for a minute. Single-file, we walked out, and the next squad filed in afterward. There was no time to loiter. There was no time for grab-ass.

In the locker room, people jumped into their duty uniforms as fast as possible to form up and march to the chow line. I cornered Shen against a locker near the back of the room. She had already dressed when she sensed my presence and turned to face me. I was inches away from her and still naked.

"You startled me," she said. A nervous smile on her face.

"What's your problem? Neither of us escaped Roundup, so why the attitude?"

She looked down for a moment. Then her eyes landed on mine. "I want you."

My face scrunched as I tried to understand what she had just said. Her dark eyes fixated on my mouth as she pulled my head down and kissed me deeply. She suddenly let go of me and hurried out to the formation. I stood there in a daze as others passed by me. I didn't make formation in time, and they put me on a week's worth of shit details, but she had kissed me.

Ioudas

8

The mess hall was long and narrow, with enough tables to seat four squads. To ensure we were hydrated, we were forced to drink a glass of water before eating any food. The food was plain and looked about the same going in as it did coming out–not the least appetizing. Our instructors didn't want us to eat more than was necessary to sustain us through our training. Nobody gained weight, and everyone stayed the same, ideal fighting size.

I faced Slik from across the table. He stirred his slop and shook his head. His voice was lowered to just over a whisper. "After two months of eating this shit, you'd think I'd develop a tolerance for it."

I swallowed my slop and tried not to taste it. It was bland and pulpy. I had no idea what it was or even what it was supposed to taste like. Glancing down the table at Shen, she returned my look with a sly smile. I grinned back at her until Slik caught me.

"You two are getting out of hand."

My smile faded. "That's none of your business."

Slik disgustedly spooned in more slop and made a bitter face while swallowing it. We finished our meal in silence. I was tired of his snide comments and didn't want to hear them anymore.

***

The armory was dark but not quiet, thanks to us. I could hear our rhythmic slapping noises echoing among lurking shells of combat armor. I could see our sweating, naked bodies reflected in the twin shell helmets along a storage wall, furiously pounding away in carnal lust. Shen was on top, bobbing back and forth until she moaned uncontrollably. I covered her mouth as she writhed. Her smothered moans eventually died out, and we switched positions, trying to get as much pleasure from each other as time permitted, knowing they could catch us at any moment.

The danger of being found out was part of the lure for us. We had consecrated our relationship in many locations around the ship and never got caught. We were pushing our luck while pushing each other to even greater heights of pleasure. Finally, we finished and collapsed in each other's arms on a bed of our clothes. The armory was cooler than any room we had done it in before, which felt good as our breath returned to normal and our sweaty bodies cooled.

Shen rested her head on my chest as it rose and fell. She looked up at me, lying with my head tilted and gazing down at her. "Do you love me, Gaven?"

I felt blood rush to my face and was thankful for the darkness.

"I love this," I admitted.

"But you feel nothing at all for me?"

I wrapped my hand across her bare butt and caressed it. She looked away, annoyed at my refusal to commit to her.

"Don't spoil the fun, Shen. In a month, we could both be dead. Then what would it matter?"

She toyed with my chest hairs for a moment. "It would mean the world to me if you said it."

I pulled her up until her face was level with mine. I kissed her deeply, and she returned the affection. Before long, we were going at it again.

***

The next day, I saw Shen being escorted by security troops into Hacker's office. She was in there until we were finished with our morning run. When we returned to our berths, I found her and asked her what had happened. She avoided me and insisted it was nothing. I didn't believe her. All I could think about was what Hacker had possibly said to her. Whatever it was, it affected her behavior towards me. She became more withdrawn and kept to herself when not in a class. I figured that somehow Hacker had found out about us and intimidated her into staying away from me. I thought about marching into his office and demanding to know, but then I realized that if he knew we were screwing around, he could use it against me, too. Possibly making things worse for both of us. I let it go for now.

***

The darkened physical training room smelled of stress-induced sweat. We were dressed in full practice armor with our Secondary Battle Arms. Alex had us attack holographic Elysian soldiers in blue and white battle armor. Most of us were getting our asses handed to us by the holographic enemy.

Polit Officer Hacker moved through our ranks, observing and shaking his head disappointingly. He was wearing the same pale blue and gray armor as the holograms. Alex wore her usual black and red combat fatigues.

"Six months in space, and most of you still can't beat a damn hologram?" Alex ranted at us.

"Of course, they can't. They're incapable of defeating us," Hacker taunted, not just us but Alex. That pissed me off more than him harassing us. I couldn't care what that man thought about anything, but when he went after Alex, he was going after our leader.

"They'll die," Hacker said with snide confidence.

Alex flashed him an irritated glare that Hacker ignored as he walked around us. He stopped to watch me fight. I was holding my own against the wavering image of the enemy soldier. My hits on the enemy flashed red where my weapon affected him. Its contact hits on me, setting off a loud buzzer.

I could feel Hacker's beady eyes watching me closely. I did my best to ignore him. Instead, I pretended the hologram was Hacker and attacked it with gusto. Red flashes across the hologram's head and shoulders registered as kill shots.

Alex approached me. "Keep your back straight. Good. I like your intensity."

I saw her look over at Hacker, who took the controller from her.

"This one's showing promise," Alex said, nodding to me.

Hacker cranked the controller settings to a higher level. "Let's see just how good he is, shall we?"

The enemy hologram charged with a renewed vigor, and I was knocked backward onto the training room floor before I knew what had hit me. That son of a bitch.

Elpida

9

My attack had knocked the bug soldier holograph onto its carapace, where I ruptured the weaker belly armor and exploded it into simulated pieces. I disengaged and returned to my ready position. Stickman moved through the smokey images of a battlefield to stand beside me. "Outstanding, Sergeant Jered. You have a genuine gift for fighting."

"I was born to kill, sir!"

Stickman shook his head and turned away from me. "Nobody's born to kill, son. Killing is a learned skill. Killing efficiently is the mark of a well-trained soldier."

"Then I shall be the best-trained soldier in the Elysian Army, sir!"

Stickman shook his head again and moved to the next combatant. "Don't flatter me. I've trained more people to kill than you've ever met. Some have returned as heroes, but most have never been heard from again."

He probably thought I was naïve, but I understood what he had said. Not everyone was cut out to be a soldier. Many, perhaps most, were not. But I knew I was truly gifted at it. I would be a survivor, and maybe, someday, I'll be in his shoes, training others to be better soldiers.

"Whether you survive will be determined by how much you want to live. Or by random chance, one or the other." Stickman laughed, amused by what he had said.

I stepped out of the sparring circle, and Saburo entered

with a nod.

"Okay, Saburo, show me what you've got," Stickman said.

Saburo assumed the ready position. He had slimmed down some around the waist, but he was still imposing. Stickman activated the holographic simulation. Two bug soldiers appeared and immediately attacked Saburo.

The big man held his own for a few minutes, a record for the rest of the recruits. Saburo dispatched one of the bug soldiers, but the second one took him down so fast he didn't know what had happened. This caused much laughter from the others as Stickman reached down to pick him up off the mat.

"Don't worry, son, the speed of combat initially overwhelms everyone. You'll get better, trust me."

***

I removed pieces of my battle armor before stepping inside the armory. There were other soldiers suiting up to enter the simulator rooms. The armory was well-lit, with mostly white walls, shiny chrome tables, and oversized chairs to accommodate those wearing armor. Each soldier had an armorer helping them dress in heavy armor. My armorer was a short young man named Jinx. The Elysian Army rarely turned down volunteers, so even if you were not tall enough to be a suit soldier, you could serve your term in space as a support technician.

Jinx and I had gotten along pretty well since they paired us up. Jinx was there to serve my every need, but we did not consider him subservient. He was an essential support crewman and highly trained in suit fitment, maintenance, and repair. A soldier would keep the same armorer even as he left the safety of the *Elpida* and entered combat on one of the Betweos moons. Armorers stayed behind at the maintenance depots and were only called into the field when there was a problem that a soldier couldn't fix himself.

"How did the bug army fare against you today, sir?" Jinx asked.

I smiled at his sardonic humor. "Not very well. Stickman says I have excellent fighting skills, though."

Jinx hunched his shoulders and said, "Mmm, the man has an unnerving ability to state the obvious sometimes."

I ignored the comment and quickly started removing my armor, handing each piece to Jinx as it came off. After several months of combat training in space, we became pretty good at donning and doffing our armor.

"You start low gravity drills tomorrow. I'll have your armor polished to perfection."

I patted him on the shoulder as he removed the final boot. "Thanks, Jinx."

Picking up one of my leg shields, I looked at it momentarily and then handed it to him. "This one came loose on me today. Can you see if you can fix it or replace it? I don't want to lose points worrying about it."

"Anything else I can do for you? Maybe speed up the ship to get to the front quicker?"

That one caused me to smile. "I'll get there soon enough."

***

I was making my way back from the simulator rooms in the longest corridor that traversed the spinning gravity wheel of the *Elpida* when a flash of light out the slit windows captured my attention. We were roughly halfway to Betweos and picking up speed with the help of the gas giant's gravity well. I stopped to look out the window and was nearly blinded by a flash of light so bright that I covered my face with my arms. When the spots began fading from my eyes, I felt the deck rumble under my feet. What the hell was that?

The entire ship shuddered for a moment. It felt as if we had hit something. Then, it dawned on me as other soldiers bolted for the next blast door. It was probably a HOM attack. Hit Or Misses were the Arachian Army's terror weapon, designed to scare us before we even got to the front. They were unguided missiles fired at every passing Elysian starship, hoping that one would get lucky and take us out or at least cause us some damage. Sometimes they were easy for the bridge crew to dodge, other times they were just drifting in space, waiting to hit a ship, like ancient sea mines.

HOMs were launched from the enemy controlled moons

of Betweos and had a limited range, so they didn't become a concern until now. The vibrations weakened until I could only feel the push of the drive. Alarms started blaring, indicating a breach in the hull. Sequential lights along the walls told us where to move to avoid being locked out by the bulkhead doors. I had never given the HOMs much thought because, realistically, the odds were against them ever hitting us. Those odds just became more accurate in my mind.

I followed the flow of traffic to the nearest bulkhead door. The *Elpida* was a warship, and as such, it had heavy blast-proof bulkhead doors designed to slam shut at the mere suggestion of a hull breach. You had literally ten seconds to get through one before it crushed you.

I made it through the door and fell on the other side. After a second jolt knocked my feet out from under me. Out of breath and with my pulse racing, I sat there looking at the door that had closed behind me. Someone reached down and pulled me to my feet. It was Selina.

"That was close, Sergeant," she said.

"I was just looking outside when I saw a flash. I think it was a HOM."

"You saw it coming?" she asked incredulously.

I dipped my head as a loud voice boomed over the PA. "Hull breach, section 407, C deck. Emergency crews en route."

Selina shook her head. "Can't be much left if it was a breach."

I grabbed her arm and urged her, "Come on, let's go see if we can help."

She didn't resist. This was the most exciting thing to happen in weeks. We ran in step to the next section of the corridor. Everyone else was moving in the opposite direction, which you're supposed to do in case another HOM has a delayed fuse. In that case, more people who were just loitering around watching the cleanup crew's work would be killed.

The main corridor angled down and turned outward. When we came around the corner at a dead run, I saw what had happened and slammed on my brakes. Selina ran into my back, and I slowed her down. Several Corpsmen were pulling the still-moving upper torso of a man who was cut in half by the blast doors. The deck was flooded with blood and entrails. I felt the bile rising in my throat immediately.

"Oh man, poor bastard," Selina said.

I became light-headed. Sweat broke out across my forehead as I looked away from the carnage. She looked at me oddly. "Did you know him?"

I shook my head, which caused my knees to start wobbling out of control.

"Hey, are you okay? You're sweating like crazy."

I purged my stomach onto the deck, and then my world started to fade as darkness cloaked me in its arms, and I passed out.

***

I was only in the infirmary long enough to get cleaned up and examined by a medical technician. He was unsympathetic as he coolly checked my vitals and made notations on his tablet. My head was perfectly clear, and my stomach was fine. I didn't even know why I was still there. "Can I go back to my unit now?"

The tech finished entering something and then looked me up and down as if he were passing judgment on me. Which, unfortunately, for me, was his job.

"How do you feel, Sergeant Jered?" he asked.

"I feel fine, I swear."

He eyed me as if I were not being completely honest with him.

"Look, this isn't going on my record, is it?"

He shook his head as if that were something everyone asked him.

"Not unless it becomes a pattern. You may return to duty now."

***

Several squad mates gathered around me expectantly when I arrived back at berthing. They all stared at me as if I had done something wrong. I ignored them and sat at a table where several people were cleaning their weapons. Metallic parts were spread everywhere as the parts were lubricated, and we silently rebuilt our weapons. The soldier beside me was sharpening his combat knife. It was matte black with a serrated edge and a deep blood groove down the blade. It was like the type my grandfather took hunting.

The soldier ran his sharpening stone down the blade several times, and I paid little attention. I started taking my rifle apart, focusing on disassembling the delicate beam splitter. The stone slid off the knife at an awkward angle, and the soldier screamed. I jumped and then saw blood squirting from between his fingers. Backing away, I twisted my face in horror. I could feel my pulse rising, and my breath got short.

That's when I noticed the other soldiers around the table burst out laughing at me as the wounded soldier revealed a package of red condiments he had used to fake his injury.

"Very funny," I said ruefully. I pretended to laugh along with everyone for a moment, and then I picked up the soldier's knife and wrapped an arm around his neck. I had the blade to the man's throat in an instant. Everyone stopped laughing at me and stared wide-eyed at the situation. I gave no indication I wouldn't just cut the man from ear to ear.

A nearby soldier named Edak put up his hands and approached me cautiously.

"Don't do it, Jered. They were just having a little fun, that's all," he pleaded.

My eyes darted around the room like a madman. I paralyzed everyone with fear. Nobody was laughing anymore. I pulled the knife away from the man's neck and placed it on the table as I backed away with my hands up.

"So was I, man. Lighten up, you pukes."

I backed away and headed for my bunk, abandoning my rifle on the table. Edak followed me. "The extreme always makes an impression. Just be careful, man. People are watching us," Edak whispered over my shoulder.

I stopped and faced the smaller man.

"You might be making an impression on the wrong man," he said.

"What do you mean?"

"Your little cutlery demo will undoubtedly be reported to Lacithe. Something like that always goes against you in the long run."

I looked around at the other soldiers. Everyone was going about their business and no longer paying me any concern. As far as I was concerned, nobody would mess with me again for a while. However, Edak was annoying me.

"Are you implying that this will go on my record?"

"It already has, man. It goes on your record every time you report to the infirmary for anything, including a headache."

"But the med tech said it wouldn't go on my record unless it happened again."

Edak shook his head as if I were a fool. "Just watch yourself, man. That's all I'm saying."

I returned his sincere look as he walked over to his bunk. I felt someone staring at me and turned to see Selina across the aisle. She winked knowingly at me and turned away. Above her, I noticed the all-seeing electronic eye of a surveillance camera for the first time. Edak's words echoed as I climbed into my bunk and pulled out my reader.

Another communique from home had arrived. There were more messages from Trille waiting for me. I decided to break my rule and open one of her messages before training was done. I needed to hear her voice in my head. She talked about her pride in having a fiancée in the army. She mentioned the harvest and how Hector had the best numbers now that I was gone. Trille finished by describing how much she missed me and couldn't wait for me to return. The message ended with a picture of her smiling with doe eyes and blonde curls. I touched the screen and remembered the smell of her hair from the last night we stayed together. I felt my love for her swelling inside, and I took a deep breath to stave off tears as I clicked off the device. She was so very far away. I missed her more than anything from home, except for my mother's cooking. The food in the army was relentlessly tasteless.

Elpida

10

Our ship, the *Elpida*, was one of many ships that traveled from Elysia to the Betweos gas giant. They traveled an invisible trajectory to the gas giant planet resting halfway between the yellow star Suth Two and the red dwarf Suth One. Betweos had a unique double-sided sunrise shadow when seen from a close enough distance. Half of the planet was bathed in a soft, ruddy light, and the other half a normal white light, leaving a cat's pupil-shaped shadow across the middle longitudinal axis. Betweos was a cosmic oddity caused by its bizarre figure-eight orbit between the two stars.

I spent much of my free time watching the silver planet grow larger on our forward observation screens. The swirling gray clouds were more majestic and beautiful the closer we came. The largest three moons, each in their orbits, could be seen rotating around the planet daily and sometimes hour-by-hour. The smallest moon was Betwi-One, tucked in close to Betweos and ravaged by its gravitational forces. Betwi-One was a red and black moon with a constantly changing landscape of fire and lava. Betwi-Two was further out and it was gray in color and inert. Craters and ancient trenches defined the surface of the dusty lunar regolith. Much further out than the other moons was Betwi-Three. The outer moon was a frozen blue and white marble with a whisper-thin layer of atmosphere that was just enough to allow for fierce wind and snow storms.

Growing up, I was a history buff regarding the war. I had

seen all the wartime documentaries on battles that had raged on all three moons. I didn't have a favorite one. I just wanted to fight on each one. My grandfather only saw combat on Betwi-One, but I wanted to be the first to fight on all three moons. How glorious would that honor be?

The *Elpida* was an elongated starship with a rotating crew module just aft the forward weapons. Many rows of solar panels were deployed along its spine, angled to the light of the much brighter Suth Two. The ship was nearly two kilometers of integrated metal sections that contained stores and ammunition for the front lines. The stern of the ship held the glowing funnels of two nuclear-powered drives. I had built many models of transfer ships as a teenager, so I was quite familiar with how fragile they looked. I had always included dark scars from HOM attacks on my models because they looked cool. Now I realized how deadly and destructive the HOM hits could be and that no ship could survive more than a couple of such hits. Every image I could see from shipboard external cameras showed a glistening, metallic ship largely unmarred from battle scars. Perhaps after a few months in orbit of the moons, the ship would dirty up from combat.

***

I dropped by Stickman's office near the end of the duty day. We had developed a rapport over the course of my training, and I felt comfortable popping in and talking about combat-related things. I was always respectful of Stickman's time because I knew that his open-door policy wasn't extended to every soldier onboard.

Fear had been a common topic of our discussions of late. How to recognize it, work through it, and deal with its effect on my fellow soldiers. Stickman always acted as if he expected me to become a leader. He never seemed bothered by our discussions and gave me his sage advice freely while asking nothing in return except that I always remain faithful to the Warrior Creed. The army called it that, but Stickman had his word for it – Mushida.

Mushida was an ancient version of the Warrior Creed, one tied to faith and the moral obligations of men. Many long hours were spent with me listening to Stickman recite the tenets of Mushida. A warrior is honest with himself and others. A warrior is courageous, a warrior is compassionate to others, especially non-warriors, a warrior has respect for himself and his leaders, a warrior's word is everything, a warrior has honor, and a warrior is fiercely loyal to his fellow soldiers.

"Sir, I've been thinking about courage again," I said.

Stickman looked over at me with restful, knowing eyes. "You're worried you won't have the courage to fight when the time comes. You're afraid that you will freeze and wind up getting killed."

I nodded sheepishly. Some great warrior I would be if I became so paralyzed with fear that I couldn't even fight.

"Fear is a paralysis that we must all conquer. I have every confidence that you will perform well in combat. What else is on your mind? Something deeper?"

I lowered my eyes and sighed. "How will I know when I am the best fighter?"

Stickman stared at me for a while and then said, "When you no longer fear death."

I raised my eyes and met his. That sounded like suicide to me. "I don't understand."

"When you are able and willing to let yourself die to protect your fellow soldiers, you will have faced the darkness of your future."

I nodded as if I understood him when I had no idea what he meant.

"You must face the darkness of your future and accept it."

"How can death be acceptable?"

Stickman nodded knowingly as if only the best warriors had ever achieved this lofty life goal. "Death in combat, protecting your mates, is the greatest honor for a soldier. Do not fear it. Expect it. Embrace it."

"But if I die in combat, won't that benefit the enemy?"

"Sometimes a battle is lost for the war to be won."

But I wanted to live. I wanted to come home as a living hero, not in a casket as a casualty of the war. Sometimes, I just didn't get my mentor. Stickman could sense my confusion and waved for me to go and think about it.

***

My squad soon found itself in the Tactical Training Room for our first introduction to where we would be fighting. Everyone was excited to finally get a real tactical briefing instead of the training scenarios that always seemed phony and contrived to kill us. On the huge screens behind Stickman were actual battle plans on an actual moon of Betweos. All data displayed was real-time, which lent a sober reality to our briefing. Our destination was B1, or the first moon of Betweos, tucked in close to the mother gas giant.

Stickman wore his blue and white dress uniform and moved around his tiny stage like a big cat on the prowl. "Your first objective when we reach orbit will be to take on the last enemy holdouts on Betwi-One. You'll be going in to meet up with the First Field Army, the illustrious Fire Starters."

The screens changed to a giant red and white logo of twisted flames. I could feel my eyes growing wide and my pulse rate increasing. My grandfather was a Fire Starter, and now I'd be helping the same combat unit. The logo faded into images of the First Field Army soldiers blasting away at the enemy centos, as if anyone in the room were unsure of how bad-ass the unit was.

"These are veteran troops with a mighty service record that goes back before most of your grandparents were born. Don't let their prestige go to your heads. Remember your mission – kill bugs. All the bugs! There can't be so much as a flicker of infra-red on that moon that is not human."

The images behind him changed to data streams and live feeds from the battlefield. He turned to study the information for a moment before continuing.

"The attack has already started, and the Fire Starters are up to their faceplates in bug guts. By the time you guys go in, they'll be mopping up. Correction. You'll be mopping up. They'll be heading to the next moon and a new fight."

The live feeds switched to the surface of B1. It was a bleak yellow-and-orange wasteland punctuated by sulfur sprays from volcanoes and pools of fresh-flowing lava. There were more ways to buy the farm there than just fighting the enemy. Tidal forces from Betweos constantly tore at the moon's crust and churned up its magma interior.

Fine sulfur ash clung to everything and eventually got inside your gear. My grandfather used to tell me that the stench was horrible. He said that over time, the seals on his suit would let the odor of rotten eggs sneak inside to torment him. In the black skies above hung the immense silver and white clouds of Betweos itself, looming like some kind of ominous eye of God over the tiny worlds locked in its grasp.

I noticed Saburo looking at me. The big man was spooked by what he saw. I gave him a confident nod, and he replied with a weak gulp.

"Two things to remember about dueling on B1: One-eighth gravity and sulfur dust. With full combat loads, it will feel like you're wearing pillows. You won't have any difficulty getting around. You'll be wearing less armor and ammo than you've been training with. The supply chain is pretty fast there. You won't have to worry about running out of ammo."

The images fluttered, and a grainy image taken from a suit camera showed a soldier who had accidentally fired his retros too hard. His white and blue body rocketed into space like a bat out of hell. It would have been comical if it hadn't happened to some poor sap.

"Sulfur ash gets into everything, and it reeks. All of your downtime will be dedicated to cleaning your suits and equipment. Armorers will not be coming with you, so get used to policing your gear.

"There are four active volcanoes on B1. Helcone Major and Montare Cone are nearest to your position. You'll be targeting the enemy's position on Hattes Plateau. The entos love to hide in the smoky vents of the volcanoes. It no doubt reminds them of the cloudy skies of Acheron. IR's not going to work. You'll have to rely on UV and active radar contacts. Remember to look sharp and shoot straight."

The entire squad sat motionless, staring at the hellish landscape on the screens. I could tell that Stickman knew that look. It was undoubtedly one of fear and regret, and every soldier probably felt it before their first drop.

"Okay, people, get out of here and head to the Entomology Lab."

***

I wasn't looking forward to dissection day in the Entomology Lab. After my fainting spell, I was worried that I'd fall over again, and it would go on my medical record. Not to mention, it's as embarrassing as hell. I repeatedly told myself that they were not humans and that, as far as I knew, they didn't even bleed red. I never got queasy in biology class at school, so I shouldn't have to worry about entos.

All my squad members encircled a medical table in the center of the operating room. Lacithe stood before the bug corpse, dressed in white scrubs with blotches from stained yellow bug blood. There was the unmistakably horrid stench of formaldehyde coming from the body. It didn't bother me, but a few soldiers were holding their noses or starting to look piqued. If I did pass out, I doubt I would be alone.

"You are about to see the body of a male entomol or Arachian entos. He is about thirty years old by his star, which would make him eighteen years old. If you think you're going to pass out or puke, please leave the lab before doing either. If the soldier beside you suddenly drops, you had better catch him before he hits the floor and makes a mess in Doctor Knido's lab," Lacithe said.

Everyone prepared for the worst as Lacithe grabbed the metallic cover off the body and revealed the partially dissected corpse. The bug's outer shell was a deep purplish color with darker splotches in random patterns. Its innards were white and yellow, with pools of yellow blood inside the cavity. It looked like a cross between a praying mantis and a roach. Only much, much larger and infinitely more disgusting than any bug I had ever seen.

The bug's head was triangular with two large, fly-like eyes with dozens of lenses and a mandible mouth that revealed several rows of teeth and a yellow tongue frozen upwards. The torso contained three segments: an upper body section, a midriff with a second set of arms, and a lower section with two thicker legs. The feet and hands had six digits, and the arms and legs had short, black hairs that reminded me of thorns.

"Its exoskeleton was discolored because he was hit with a long burst of radiation, effectively leaving the body intact for classroom discussion," Lacithe said.

Behind us, monitors blinked on, showing the evolution of life on Acheron.

"The earliest forms of life on Acheron were thought to be no different than what we have on Elysia. There were mammals, reptiles, fish, plants, and insect species. The various species began to die off one by one as their sun faded. Eventually, only the insect species remained. The planet became enshrouded in acidic clouds that only the heartiest bugs could thrive in."

The other species fell away, and various bug species merged and evolved until they were very similar to what we had before us.

"Out of this hellish environment came the Entosentients, the intelligent insects. The result of this evolutionary chain is what you see before you, a human-sized, fully sentient bug whose government has been waging war with humans for over two hundred years."

The screens went dark, and everyone's attention fell back to the body on the metal table before them. Lacithe moved around the corpse. Harsh operating room lights from above illuminated his blue hair and cast shadows across his pale face.

"That rotting stench is what they smell like after being irradiated. If you could get a whiff of how they smelled, you'd all be hurling right now."

Someone near the back heaved their lunch onto the floor almost on command. I looked in the direction of the sound and locked eyes with Selina. She didn't look disturbed by the body or the puke. She rolled her eyes dismissively as if she didn't believe Lacithe's words.

***

It wasn't long afterward that the *Elpida* started braking for B1 orbit. We would be making our first combat jump in a few short days. Tensions were higher than normal, and many soldiers kept more to themselves. I noticed that Saburo had begun withdrawing from his usual go-lucky self. Death was more and more on everyone's mind, not just our mortality but that of our friends and squad mates. It started to feel like death was an amorphous, silent stalker lurking out there in the darkness of space, waiting to take random victims.

Many turned to their religions and were constantly attending services or mumbling mantras to ward off death or to somehow make their lives more palatable to whichever deity had the power to save them. I was never religious and didn't spend my time alone or in the chapel. I preferred to clean my weapon and listen to my music. Like an athlete preparing for a big game, I saw myself as an invincible winner. I focused on memorizing combat formations and spent more time than the others looking at the latest intelligence from the battlefield.

When it came to maintaining my weapons, I was nothing short of anal in my attention to detail. I often pointed out mistakes others were making, even as my weapon functioned flawlessly. Stickman noticed and often used my knowledge to explain things to the slower soldiers.

"You're doing it wrong. The bolt has to sit in the groove easily; you can't force it," I said to Selina, the only soldier working near me.

She pulled her bolt out and wiggled it into position again. This time, it went in easily.

"Thanks, punk."

I removed my headphones and started wiping down my weapon. I looked over at her and watched her work for a moment. She became self-conscious of my stare and looked up.

"What?"

"Nothing. You're doing fine."

"Then mind your own business," she said, her tone reflecting her increasing nervousness at going into battle.

I held up a defensive hand and studied my weapon. My focus slowly went back to Selina. Her dark eyes were laser-focused on assembling her weapon. She glanced over at me again, and I looked away in an overly exaggerated manner.

"Are you afraid of dying on your first drop?" She asked.

I stopped trying to avoid eye contact with her and cracked a sideways grin. "Heck no. I can't wait to get down there and waste some bugs."

She studied me this time. I could feel her stare as I did my business, snapping the return and patting the rifle with an oil-soaked rag.

"Everyone's afraid of dying, Jered."

"Not me."

She put down her weapon and faced me. "Why the hell not?"

I set my weapon down gently. "This is all just a big adventure. I mean, the odds favor us more on this drop than any other. We're just mopping up the leftovers. Nobody's going to die this time, Selina."

She marveled at my confidence. "I hope you're right," she said.

I winked at her. "Someday, we'll tell our grandkids about this."

Selina shook her head and picked up her next weapon to clean. I had already started taking apart my second weapon. I was finished before she had removed the first section of hers. I brushed the carbon off the blued metal pieces with a cleaning pad. The rhythmic motions were similar to a person's swaying while reciting a mantra. My way of coping with the stress, I guess.

"I only wish I knew the truth about why we're fighting. This whole bug war crap is a facade," Selina said.

I stopped cleaning and looked directly at her. I brought my finger to my lips to silence her. I looked around to see if anyone had overheard what she had said. Everyone was pretty self-absorbed and didn't react.

"Are you crazy?"

"No. I believe in the ancient prophecies that claim the birthplace of our species is Acheron."

My face wrinkled with revulsion as she spoke. "You better not talk about that crap around me, soldier! I plan to make something of my service, and I won't be dragged into treasonous talk by you or anyone else."

Selina looked around suspiciously and then leaned in closer to me.

"Come on, aren't you the least bit curious? Didn't that bug corpse look fake to you? I mean, you didn't even get squeamish."

I pulled back from her. "I don't get squeamish over dead bugs."

She smiled back at me and mouthed, "Bug. Myth."

I stood up fast, my blood pressure rising. Slamming my receiver down hard on the table, I walked away. I didn't have to sit there and listen to that crap from her.

***

I had heard the rumors about the Bug Myth but never believed them. It was all just double-speak propagated by the anti-war camp. There was no evidence to back up their claim. None.

I wouldn't have given it much thought if it wasn't for who had said it. There was something about Selina; I just couldn't get her out of my head. She wasn't particularly beautiful or an amazing soldier. Maybe her dark black eyes made her more mysterious than anyone I had ever seen. When she looked at me, I could feel her penetrate me to my bones. It was unnerving, but I liked it.

Maybe it was her prematurely gray hair that had hints of violet in it under the fluorescent light of the ship. I had never seen anyone with hair as gray as hers who was essentially the same age as me. She was both exotic and intriguing at the same time. My inner voice raged against my attraction. She's a temptress! Out to convert me to her treasonous ways! I knew I should avoid her if I were going to keep my wick and my soul clean from her wicked influence. Still, she was there, and I was only human.

I could reason all kinds of ways to break my vows to Trille. She would never find out about my lapse in loyalty because there was a good chance one or both of us would die in combat. Hell, we could all lose this battle.

That's when the nervous twitching started to show itself in my right hand. I didn't notice it then, but others around me did, and they all wrote it off as pre-battle nerves. But I was not nervous about fighting or the possibility of losing my life. Throwing away the trust and faith placed in me by Trille for the easy, here-and-now of Selina was what frightened me.

In the days leading up to our first drop, I distanced myself from Selina. She noticed, but I didn't care. I had to focus on the coming battle and get my mind in the game again. I was not letting my libido and curiosity about her drive my thoughts and actions into getting me in trouble. I stayed in the simulation rooms longer and teamed up with Saburo more, keeping my mind off her.

Coming out of the mess hall the night before our drop, she pushed me into an empty training room and shut the hatch behind her. I was immediately concerned, but I stayed calm. Her eyes drilled into my chest and penetrated my shields.

"Why the hell have you been ignoring me lately?"

I mumbled something that she didn't hear.

"What?"

I turned away and moved as far away from her as I could get.

"Look, I don't have time for this. We drop tomorrow, and I must keep my mind clear and sharp."

"What the hell does that mean?" she pressed.

I looked down at my hand and noticed it shaking for the first time. I grasped it with my other hand to calm it.

"I, I'm just nervous, alright."

"What? You are nervous. Are you kidding me? You don't get nervous about fighting or dying. Remember?"

I watched her slowly move closer to me, fake concern etched on her face. "I think we better take you to the infirmary. You might be sick or something."

I nervously laughed off the comment.

"Look, I've been thinking about what you said about the war not being legit. I don't believe you. I think you're trying to mess with my head or something, and I won't have it."

Her expression turned to pity as she shook her head slowly.

"Look, man, I was messing with you. Forget it, alright?

Just go out there tomorrow and blast away at them damn bugs like they're nothing but giant roaches. Don't worry yourself about whether you're killing men in mechanical suits."

Her sarcasm hit home, and I started to stand up straighter. My hand stopped shaking. This was not about me and her. This was about her stupid theory, not anything she felt for me.

I reached out and pushed her away as I left the room. The heavy blast hatch slammed shut behind me, signaling my freedom. Bring on the damn bug army. I'm ready for them.

Ioudas

11

The final few weeks of our training seemed to slip away in the blink of an eye. Alex rode us hard and didn't give us time to consider our rapid approach to Betweos. This was, of course, intentional, and it never failed to work in her favor. My mates and I were not thinking about what would happen to us in combat, only whether we would make it to the next training phase.

Alex gathered us in a cramped classroom again. After a few minutes of quiet, she called the room to attention, and Polit Officer Hacker strode to the front of the room wearing his dress reds. His red hair was spiked to perfection, and his uniform was crisp and tight.

The screen behind him lit up with images from the battlefield. It was our first look at where we would be fighting. Betwi-One was an actively volcanic world. Betwi-Two had gray regolith flats with no atmosphere, and Betwi-Three was a frozen ball of ice and snow. The focus of his lecture, though, was not on where we would be fighting; it was on who we'd be fighting.

"The enemy takes no prisoners. They will kill you if you try and surrender, so don't even bother. Many troopers have tried to defect in the heat of combat, and all of them were killed in cold blood by Elysian soldiers. So if you've been planning on switching sides to get out of fighting for Acheron, do what you can afford."

Nobody I knew had ever spoken about defecting before.

Not even I had considered it, which was a drastic oversight on my part. I was always thinking about how to get out of fighting so that I could survive long enough to return. Now that I knew they took no prisoners, it looked like a pretty dumb move regardless.

"Just because the enemy doesn't take prisoners doesn't mean we don't. We most certainly do take prisoners. If any Elysian soldiers try to defect or give up, you are duty-bound to disarm them and return them to the rear echelons. Where they will be processed, debriefed, and retrained to fight for our side, they won't get out of fighting, but they will do so for us."

I raised my hand, and Hacker nodded to me.

"Sir, what if they refuse to fight their own kind?"

Hacker looked around the room and ran a finger across his neck. He then went over all the disarming procedures and took them back for processing. It seemed to me like a good way to get out of the line of fire and still be doing your job. I wondered if you could score a rear-echelon position guarding prisoners. That would be one surefire way to stay alive long enough to win a free home trip. I filed that plan away for future reference.

Later that day, when we were afforded some free time in billeting, Shen and I sat together at a table, cleaning our training rifles. I waited until nobody was in earshot and whispered my plan to get on prisoner detail at some point.

"I don't think you get to pick assignments like that," she said.

"Maybe not, but they always ask for volunteers, and nobody ever raises their hand because it usually involves some crap details. But when we're on station, a crap detail might buy you some time away from the fighting. Which increases your odds of going home alive."

Shen conceded that as she wiped down her weapon with an oily rag. We continued cleaning until she spoke again. "Gaven, what will you do if I get killed before you? Will you still try and get back home?"

I looked at her and shrugged. "Probably. What about you?"

"Same."

I slid the last piece of my rifle into place and locked it down. "Do you think Hacker ever goes into combat?"

Shen glanced up with a slightly startled look. "Ah, doubtful. I don't even think Sergeant Alex fights anymore."

I shook my head ruefully. "Too bad, man. Too damn bad."

Shen's dark eyes were big as she watched me shoulder my weapon. I wanted to kill Hacker. Hell, everyone did on some level. I could tell by the way she looked at me that she knew I wanted to kill him more than anyone else.

***

The next day, Alex had us in our Secondary Battle Arms again; this time, we were going over how we coordinated in battle. The suits were controlled by a sophisticated software package concealed on our packs for maximum protection in combat. It was complicated technology that even Alex barely understood on anything other than a superficial level.

She went over procedures to restart what she called the Brains Package whenever it froze, which, according to her, was more often than not. As advanced as the SBAs were, they were simple to maintain in combat. Each sub-system was removable and easily replaced with a completely new module whenever it acted up or was damaged. Alex kept repeating the mantra, Stop, Swap, and Pop, which she applied to just about any question on how to fix the system.

"Sarge, what if the Life Support package blows out on you," I asked.

"You have two minutes to – wait for it – Stop, Swap, and Pop a new module into place. Everyone carries a spare module for the Brain and Life Support packages. These modules are not unique to your suits. So, if you can remove a module from a dead trooper, then maybe you won't join them in the afterlife. Understand?"

The room shouted, "Yes, Sergeant!"

Alex had us practice Stopping, Swapping, and Popping a new module into place over and over again. Then she had us do it for our battle buddy. It was not complicated, but she needed it to be second nature for us, or the army would unnecessarily lose troopers to equipment failures.

Once everyone had mastered changing modules, she started getting deeper into the technical stuff, making squad leaders responsible for their squadmates' health and welfare. The suits had a diagnostic cord that could be pulled out of a leader's suit and plugged into another person's suit to run tests and troubleshoot errors. Menus with yes or no answer trees quickly isolated which module was bad and needed replacing.

Before long, our squad leaders were fully trained to diagnose and fix simple problems without requiring their troopers to leave the fight. I enjoyed learning about how the SBAs worked. I had a knack for picking up technology. I might have been an engineer if I hadn't been born a Topper.

***

Small arms training seemed like a waste of time to me. Hardly anyone used pistols in suit armor, much less knives and hand-to-hand combat. The days spent with Alex in the gym reviewing how to disarm someone both in your SBAs and outside them were long and boring.

It wasn't like I was always getting the upper hand on her or one of my squad mates because I was no better at it than anyone else. She sensed that I was bored and tried to come at me with different tactics than she had taught in class. I was able to counter her just about every time.

"How did you get so good at this, Gaven?" Alex asked after I had just tossed her on her butt for the second time in a row.

"The surface of Acheron is a rough place, Sergeant. I know all your Roundup tricks and've spent a lifetime defending myself from other gangs. Thugs don't play fair, and you don't normally get a second chance."

She seemed impressed by my answer as she got to her feet. Circling me for a minute, she decided on another attack vector – my mind. "Hacker doesn't think you're anything special, you know?"

"Whatever. He also thinks he can control me, so he's already lost."

She shook her head. If she only knew how deep my hatred went for that man.

I motioned for her to come at me again instead of circling. She put her hands up in defeat and slowly approached me. We were both sweating, and she wiped her brow as I stared at her with rock-steady eyes.

"Do you ever fear anything? Combat injuries? Dying? Maybe snakes?" she asked.

I snorted at the weak attempt at humor. Alex smiled at me, but her smile faded quickly, and she pressed me again. "Well, what do you fear?"

I sniffed and looked away from her to consider the question honestly. In that split second, she landed a punch to my chin. It was a powerful jab, and it sent a tooth flying from my jaw along with a splatter of blood and sweat. I slowly turned around to face her. I could taste the copper of my blood as I locked eyes with her. I slowly looked down, and she followed my gaze.

I had positioned my pistol so that it rested against her side. The pistol was an inert trainer, painted red and made from ballistic plastic. It had a functioning slide on it, and I pulled the trigger, sending the slide forward along the top of the barrel, where it cracked her rib with a loud snap that caused the other troopers to look at us.

Alex felt the sting of the rib breaking, but she didn't fall. Her ability to move was completely affected by the broken rib, and she didn't retaliate.

"I don't like surprises," I muttered just above a whisper.

Alex nodded slowly. It was the only thing she could move that didn't hurt like hell. A buzzer rang, and everyone left the room for the next class, muttering under their breaths about Alex and I's fight.

"Get to the infirmary and have that tooth fixed," Alex said, without breathing.

I picked up my tooth from the floor and headed for the door. I could hear her exhaling slowly as she fell to her knees in pain behind me.

Ioudas

12

The final phase of training was called the Black Phase. We noticed a distinct change in the attitudes and intensity of our instructors. We were treated almost as if we were real people instead of maggots, as Alex called us. Now, she referred to us as larvae or trainees when she was in a good mood.

One of the benefits of this newfound humanity was one-on-one meetings with Alex concerning our training status. She would meet with individuals in her small office just off the squad berthing. Most of the regular recruits probably talked about their fears of looming combat. But I wasn't like most troopers, and Alex was well aware of that.

"How's your rib, sergeant?" I asked cheekily.

She looked at me for a moment. "Fine. How's the tooth?"

"I didn't need it."

She knew damn well the doctors had replaced my tooth, and I had missed a few days of training because of it. If anyone could have afforded to miss training it was me. I led the squad in every area that was scored. But this meeting was about what we weren't graded on. It was about the intangibles, like the heart and soul of a trooper. It was the one thing she knew I didn't want to talk about.

"So, how are you doing, Gaven? Any troubles this week with your training?"

"Nope."

We could relax all the snappy yes sergeant bullshit during our private meetings with her. No doubt designed to put us at ease so we would spill our guts.

She looked down at her screen and pushed around some data. "Your marksmanship is the best in the squad. It's better than the whole platoon."

I didn't react—I never did—when she told me of my successes. It was only when she brought up areas for improvement that I started to get defensive with her. In my mind, I was perfect, and who the hell was she passing judgment on, anyway?

"I saw you helping another recruit carry his load on the endurance course yesterday."

I lifted an eyebrow. Where the hell was she going with that?

"Are you going to carry the load of others in combat?" she asked.

"No. But this is training, not the real thing."

I just knew she would throw that back at me, and she didn't disappoint.

"We train like we fight."

I conceded that one to her.

"Gaven, you've been helping others to survive all of your life, am I correct?"

I didn't react, but she could tell I was thinking about what she had said. "You were a gang leader back on the surface. Others looked up to you and depended on your abilities to keep them alive. That's not an easy burden for a young man."

I shifted in my chair. "I was okay with it."

She studied me for a moment before returning to her notes. "In combat, you won't be able to save everyone. Your people will die, and there won't be a damn thing you can do about it. War is ruthlessly random when it comes to who lives and who dies. You can control the fight to some extent, but you will take hits sooner or later, and one of them could be your friend."

I must have rolled my eyes, and she noticed it.

"You can't scare me with the randomness of the war, or

the fucking universe, or whatever you're trying to do."

She sat back and raised her hands defensively. "I'm only trying to make you a better trooper, son. I'm not trying to get in your head."

I sat back in my chair and folded my arms defensively. That's exactly what she was trying to do.

"I need to know that you won't freeze up and become a liability when your friends are dying around you. We send you people into hell with the best weapons and armor that we can make, but if you go psycho on us, all of that money and time is wasted. Can you understand now why we're so concerned about your mental health?"

I nodded. Fair enough.

"Okay. Get the hell out of my office, trooper."

I picked myself up from the chair and left without saying another word. I was convinced she was either scared of my abilities or thought I was going to snap. Either way, I had her guessing, which was to my advantage because whatever she saw got reported to Hacker in the end.

***

A section of the *Ioudas* was dedicated to the gravity wells of the three moons we would fight on. Most were about one-sixth that of Acheron, but Betwi-One was different. It was significantly smaller and troopers had to sometimes use retro rockets to jet around its fiery lava features.

Alex had us train under this lowered gravity exclusively in our SBAs. It took us several hours to move like oversized balloons from side to side instead of in a straight line, which messed with our aim when shooting. Our training weapons were modified to shoot paintballs so we could see the effects of the lower gravity on the rounds they shot and compensate for it. Some of us caught on quickly, and others struggled with everything from moving to laying down suppressive fire.

Alex made the element leaders into her assistants so we could work in smaller groups of four instead of twenty-four. I was the First Element leader, and Slik was the Second Element leader. The Third Element leader failed to grasp the low gravity fundamentals and Alex quickly replaced him with Shen. This was no accident on Alex's part. She knew we all came from the same roundup and were quite familiar with each other. Some of us were more familiar than others; nothing escaped her notice. She hoped the unit would work as a team better than any other combination of her troopers. She was not wrong.

The entire squad made it through the low-gravity block training in record time. We had the best marksman scores, maneuvering scores, and the quickest times in and out of individual training. Even Hacker was impressed with our progress, and that damn near never happened.

***

The final stretch of the Black training phase was combat patrols and tactics. I thought they would have spent more time on this before now, and in a way, they had. This was where they got us to bring everything we had been learning to bear in one series of exercises that simulated actual attack strategies and defensive tactics.

We were fully suited up in our training SBAs and armed with real weapons modified to shoot harmless IR beams. Specially applied patches across our amour registered hits. They looked like bit-mapped camouflage on the gray battle suits. Attack orders were issued once we got into the arena, gravity was set to simulate Betwi-One and computer-generated environments were fed to our suit cameras, making it look like we were on the moon. This was the first time we had trained in full suits, and everyone found it a bit disorienting. Many of us wondered why they waited this long to get realistic.

Alex was not with us for these exercises. She and Hacker were in a control room, pulling the strings for the simulation. They could talk to us but could not give us advice and would only stop the simulation if someone was in physical danger.

"Alright, larvae, you're on your own now. Just like you will be in two weeks. I'm done holding your hands and cleaning up your little messes. Squad leaders, execute your orders," Alex's voice boomed.

I was the squad leader for this one. A big guy from another group named Prome was responsible for our opposing force. Introducing a new leader was one of the exercise parameters so we just had to deal with it. When we got into actual fights, we would filter in with already established units, and our current formation would no longer exist. So it was imperative that we be able to adjust and work with a new team.

The mission objective was only shown to me. As the leader, it was up to me to move my squad around as I saw fit to achieve the objective. In this case, the objective was to capture a "flag" behind the enemy lines—simple enough.

Thirty minutes into the mission, we were within sight of the flag. We had only lost one trooper to enemy fire. I held everyone up around the flag barricade and considered my next move. We had been still until my comms lit up with Alex's voice.

"What's the delay? Engage, Black Force, engage!"

I ignored her. I couldn't switch frequencies or adjust the volume, so I just tuned her out the best I could and tried to consider what the enemy would do when they attacked. We were going up against Hacker's team, so I knew whatever happened would be extreme and would probably kill all of my people, including me.

What weapon does the enemy have that could take out my whole squad? I asked myself. I cycled through the inventory in my head as other troopers started complaining that we were not moving. I tuned them out, too. The worst thing in the enemy inventory was a battlefield EMP burst. The Acheron Army called them EMPers, and when the enemy set them off, it would use an Electromagnetic Pulse to neutralize all the electronics within the immediate area of the discharge. They were not used very often and were crude to aim, meaning there was a general risk to both the user and his prey.

I started issuing orders, and my people began to form two lines to attack. I positioned myself between the flag barrier and three rows of suited troopers leading the attack.

We met little resistance at first. Then, a few blue-and-white-dressed Elysian soldiers emerged and were quickly dispatched by my first row. As we got within meters of the barrier, Hacker stepped out and held up an EMPer. He immediately discharged it, and nothing seemed to happen.

I was well hidden behind three other suited troopers. My screens went dark, flickered, and then popped back online with a loud burst of static. All of my troopers were immobilized as their suits came to a halt, and all their life support systems shut down. My scanners indicated that everyone was dead except for me.

Hacker was wearing a lightly armored Elysian battle suit as he walked past the rows of immobilized Acheron Army troopers. When he reached me, he stopped and checked his own scanners, surprised to see that I was still alive.

"Congratulations, Private Gaven. You've killed your entire squad," Hacker said.

I pulled the trigger on my rifle and set off the kill alert on Hacker's armor.

"I win."

***

After the exercise, Alex and Hacker convened in their office. I removed my helmet and could hear them shouting at each other. My squad stayed in their suits and waited for Alex to return for the debriefing. A few were miffed that I had sacrificed them to win, but all of them understood that the EMPer would have killed them all no matter what I had done.

Finally Alex came out and pointed at me to come inside. Shit.

Hacker was furious. His cheeks were redder than normal, and his black eyes were open wide. Alex was calmer, and I got the sense that she was somehow proud of what I had done.

"You're the first to have beaten that exercise," Hacker admitted between his clenched teeth. "But you killed everyone in your squad doing it."

I glanced at Alex, who urged me to speak.

"They were going to die anyway. I knew you were going to use the EMPer," I glanced back at Alex, whose lips were slowly parted in a grin.

Facing Hacker, I said, "I'll do whatever it takes to win, sir."

Alex's smile slipped away. She knew I was replying to her accusation that I was too protective of my people. My message was received.

Elpida

13

Drop day had finally arrived. Everyone in my platoon was abnormally quiet and withdrawn as if they were contemplating the meaning of life before it was ripped from them like a flower by the stem. Everyone, that is, except for me. I was filled with barely contained anticipation. This was the day I'd been dreaming about ever since I was a kid when I reenacted the battlefield heroics of my grandfather in the dirt of the corn fields. I had a wooden gun in my cold hands as I stomped on the frozen puddles between the rows of plowed corn stalks, crushing ice under my boots like the carapaces of enemy bugs.

Today, I would become a battle-hardened army veteran, defending Elysia from the horrid Bug Army of Acheron. Today, I would test my ability against the best the enemy could throw at me and defeat them. Today would be a day long remembered by the leaders of both armies. It would be the day I entered the war and changed the outcome forever.

We were all suited up and encased inside the launch tubes that would jettison us down to the surface of B1. The drop room was dim. The only light came from Stickman's helmet spot as he checked every man and woman. Twin beams of red light bathed the clear tube inside when Stickman stood before a soldier.

As I waited to be checked, my eyes scanned the virtual instruments projected onto the inside of my faceplate. My pulse was up but not too high. My core temperature was slightly down, but I didn't feel cold. Life support indicators were all green. Ammunition was full, and all weapons were green. Incoming data from the surface battle were updating my maps on troop strength and enemy positions. Those First Army troops were tearing them up down there, and I wanted to join them before it was all over.

I could see Stickman move before Selina and listen to their exchange over my breathing. He was reminding her to keep her weapon barrel down in the low gravity, something he told every soldier multiple times, and thus, they all heard it numerous times. She responded with a clear affirmative in her clipped manner that I found so irritating yet so enticing simultaneously.

Stickman moved down the line to Saburo, who was right beside me. Saburo was nervous as the Training NCO gave him the visual once over. I could hear my friend's heavy breathing as clearly as if I were inside his armor instead of mine.

"Relax, soldier, you're about to get your first kill. Don't forget to savor the moment," Stickman said to him.

Saburo responded with a quivering voice followed by a forced sigh. I smiled to myself. I didn't expect the big man to be so scared. He had performed brilliantly in all the combat training we had endured together.

Stickman's dual red lamps flashed in my eyes as he stood before me. I avoided staring into the light but couldn't quite see the man's dark eyes behind the layers of clear armor.

"Take charge, Sergeant Jered. Get these people into the entrance, and don't let them linger outside and get wasted. Copy?"

"Hoo-rah, sir!"

Stickman pressed his face closer so that I could see him. "Get some, kid. I can't wait to read your After Action Report."

The *Ioudas* rotated and lurched a few times as we approached the moon. Warning messages flashed across my helmet screens. The ship was under heavy enemy fire as it maneuvered into position to eject us.

Stickman finished his squad review and took hold of a

loose strap against the gray walls of the drop room. He would not be going with us. Our squad leader would be Carine. She was in the last group to punch out. Until she arrived on target, I would be in charge. It was a great honor for me to be in command, even for so short a time. I trembled slightly in anticipation. Let's get this show on the road!

**

My mind drifted in the interminable time it took to position the ship for our launch. I thought of Selina and saw her face. It morphed into the innocent face of Trille. I had forgotten how stunning her big blue eyes were. How much they looked like the color of the Elysian flag. The sweet cinnamon taste of her breath. The way she squealed when she came and dug her nails into my back. Cut it out, soldier!

That's when the bottom fell out, and I was shot feet first into the fiery skies over Betwi-One. My pod shook violently from nearby flak explosions. The outside temperature became blindingly hot as the pod burned away, and my reentry streamer exploded above my head. I could see the curvature of the moon and the thin, useless atmosphere glisten as I augured my way to the red lava streams below.

The suit retro rockets kicked in, slowing me enough to prevent my legs from breaking when I slammed into the hardened lava surface. I rolled over and slid to a stop into a sulfur sand pile near the drop zone. Breathing hard from the thrill ride, I came to rest flat on my back, staring up at the sky from where I had fallen. The thin clouds did little to block out the stars of space and the massive form of Betweos that dominated the sky.

I grabbed the ground, feeling like I would fall into the swirling silver and white clouds of the gas giant in the sky. But I didn't fall. I was at the mercy of the slightly lower gravity of the moon. Inky clouds from exploding shells dotted the sky. Static bursts flooded my ears with the sounds of battle. I was back in the fight.

Someone offered me a gloved hand, and I took it, bouncing upright with no effort at all. It was Edak. "C'mon, the entrance is that way," he said, pointing to a black crevice in the nearest lava tube outcrop.

I hoisted my rifle and followed Edak. Others landed around us and haphazardly skidded across the ground. We ran to the new arrivals and helped them up. I reached down and pulled up Saburo. He was grimacing from pain, but I didn't see where he was hit.

"Are you alright?" I asked.

"I'm fine. Where's Carine?"

"I don't think she made it down."

"Shit, man. Who's in charge then?"

We looked at each other for a moment. Our leader hadn't made it down. That didn't bode well for the attack. I was the highest-ranking soldier in our platoon. I straightened up and took the lead. No fear, no hesitation.

"Let's go, follow me."

I pushed off and started bounding for the entrance of the lava tube. Saburo and I glanced over our shoulders and saw the rest of our platoon falling like metal hail. The flak chewed up many of them and fell into smaller pieces. For a moment, it rained glittery shards of metal and bloody body parts.

Under the cover of the lava tube, we watched a single soldier running across the graveyard. I recognized Bree by her gait and her ammo load. She slid into the tube in a cloud of sulfur dust as a shell hit behind her.

The four of us—Saburo, Edak, Bree, and I—spread out and activated our IR scanners. My HUD took on an eerie red and black glow, and I could see further into the cavern's dark recesses.

"Targets acquired, four marks ahead," Edak said behind clenched teeth. "Time to play."

He headed down the tube, taking point, his plasma rifle at the ready, sweeping the area. I waved for Saburo to follow and then Bree. I took up the rear with a casual glance across the landing zone for any stragglers. It was quiet as a graveyard on comms.

Edak and Saburo had already rounded a bend out of sight when I heard them engaging the enemy. The only sound came from their intercom traffic, which was filled with excited commands and flashes of brilliant light from their weapons.

"Get down!"

"I got one!"

"Two more on the left."

By the time Bree and I rounded the curve, the show was over. Edak was down, and Saburo was hovering over the inert body. Bree took a position ahead of them, searching for new enemy targets.

Saburo motioned to our dead comrade, "They nailed him before I could see them. But it looks like he took one of them with him."

I patted him on the back. "We'll come back for him. Right now, we have to keep moving."

Saburo hoisted his rifle, and we continued down the lava tube. After a few meters, the tube opened to the bright outside light. Pointing our rifles up, looking for contacts, we edged around the hole and continued down the tube. It started to descend, and fresh lava ran off to our left, segmenting as it hardened.

"Multiple contacts ahead. No idea who," Bree said from point.

"Make sure they're not ours. We're supposed to be relieving the First."

Bree turned back to look a Saburo for a split second. That was all the enemy bug needed to laze off her head and shoulders with a green plasma beam.

I saw it happen and felt my anger rising as I charged my rifle and opened up on several four armed soldiers moving nearby. Plasma bolts crisscrossed the narrow lava tube for what seemed like forever until I was knocked backward by concussion grenades. Saburo returned fire above me, giving me cover as I gathered my head and scrambled up. I could hear noise over my comm but couldn't understand it. My ears were still ringing like bells in a choir.

Saburo pointed off to the right, and I saw several muzzle flashes. Lava rock exploded above us, raining shiny black metal splinters atop us. We had to move, or we'd be buried alive.

I activated my thrusters and shot out ahead, my helmet scraping the top of the lava tube. I fired down at the gray armored bugs, taking them out. My rifle jammed open and the resulting concentration of fire blew out the side of the lava tube and opened up a new tunnel before I slammed into the hard wall of the tube. I never felt it when I hit the ground. I was already out cold.

***

When I came to, I slowly focused on the mission's elapsed time—only a few minutes had passed. Good, hopefully, I didn't miss much. That was a pretty stupid move on my part.

My ears were still ringing, but I could understand comm traffic. I brushed off shards of lava rock and got to my feet. New contacts registered on my screens ahead. I checked my rifle and saw that it was drained. I must have expended the whole power pack when it had jammed.

Saburo came to my side and watched as I reloaded.

"That was fucking awesome, man! You took out that group and blasted a hole in the tube. I think we've caught the buggers by surprise."

I motioned down the new tube with my rifle. "More contacts that way."

Saburo took the point, and several other Elysian troopers moved past. I had no idea where they had come from, but I was glad to have their firepower. I filed in behind them and checked my six. Broken bodies of Arachian soldiers lay scattered around where I had blasted them. They were melted into the rock and metal in a steaming pile of charred debris. Their amber blood splattered all over their armor and the burnt lava ground. I noticed what I thought was a femur bone sticking out of one of the bug's legs. I blinked a bead of sweat and refocused. Surely, that was part of the exoskeleton. Before I could refocus on it, my attention was thwarted by renewed fighting.

Saburo and the others had opened fire again on more enemy soldiers. When I made it up to them, their newly acquired SAW gunner had taken a full frontal hit from enemy fire. He staggered backward into my arms, stunned by the impacts.

"He's taken a beating. His armor is depleted," a familiar voice said. It was Selina. I hadn't noticed her pass me before.

I hoisted the man back up, and he shook his head to clear it.

"I'm alright, it just startled me, is all. I still have as many layers as you guys," the gunner said. His nameplate read Jamis.

"He's right, plus we need his firepower," I said, letting the man go back into position. Selina stared coldly at me as I passed.

The five of us pressed down the newly discovered lava tube tunnel for a few more klicks before I began seeing the light up ahead. I tapped another soldier to be the tail and moved past Selina and the SAW gunner to where Saburo was.

"Targets ahead, but I think they're friendlies," Saburo offered.

I analyzed my screens and came to the same conclusion. I hadn't seen friendly signals since we had landed. Nothing but red enemy signals from the moment we cleared the landing zone.

A low-lying sulfur mist blew in from just ahead of us. Saburo and I exchanged concerned looks. It wasn't from weapons fire. It must have been from the planet's active veins. We pressed on, weapons at the ready.

The lava tube opened into a huge cavern big enough to house a platoon or more soldiers. The helmet lights on our suits would not have provided enough light to see the whole cavern. Light carts from the Elysian Army were placed around the cavern, pointing up to bounce their light down on the dozen battle-scarred Fire Starter troops.

Their blue and gray armor was pockmarked with blasts and dusted with sulfur. The paint was worn off metal armor along the edges. Smoke drifted from their helmets like condensing steam on a hot runner's head. These were the best of the best in the Elysian Army. Saburo and I could only stare in awe at them. They had survived countless days in the fight and were still ready and willing to dish it out.

A seasoned LT approached us. I had to force myself not to salute in a combat zone. The man put a hand on my shoulder armor.

"Are you our replacements?" he asked. His voice couldn't hide his amusement.

"Yes, sir! Echo squad, fourth platoon," I answered.

The lieutenant shook his sweaty, bearded face inside his helmet. Dark patches under his weary eyes indicated that he had probably not slept for more than ten minutes at a time in a week.

"Congratulations, you're the first to make it in."

Saburo and I exchanged astonished looks. Of all the soldiers who dropped, we were the first to arrive. Only five out of fifty made it? I started to wonder if anyone else would ever show up.

"Power's over there. Pull up a rock and get your gear cleaned. More from your platoon should be here shortly. At least, I hope so, for your sake."

The LT grimaced and moved back to his group of soldiers. I waved the others in our group over to the power hookups. I counted six of us—not even a full squad.

"He didn't even ask what happened to our sergeant," I noted aloud.

"Like he cares. You'll probably get a promotion. You're the highest ranking," Saburo said.

Selina approached, then stopped, giving me the eye. I smirked at her and said, "Any confirmed kills, Private?"

"Three, Corporal. Yourself?"

"Five, I think. Lost count."

Saburo laughed. "I got eight."

Selina and I shook our heads as Saburo motioned for us to look back the way we had come. Four new stragglers were walking in, looking up in amazement at the expansive cavern.

"Damn, that can't be everyone?" I asked rhetorically.

Each of them had a different-colored armband, indicating they were all from different squads of Fourth Platoon. There was not an NCO among them, either. They were just another bunch of privates stranded by the confusion of war.

"So much for the easy Drop and Mop mission," I said.

"Down on the moons, the survival rate is two days," Saburo said, quoting the recruiter we had met at the departure point on Elysia. "Guess he was right after all."

I welcomed the new guys over with a wave. A dark-eyed

woman whose nameplate read Geena noticed my rank and addressed me. "We thought we were the only ones to survive."

"Fall in with our squad. Anyone else behind you?"

She shook her head inside her helmet. "We got pinned down outside, and they cut our squad to pieces. Damned slaughter out there."

I nodded in agreement with her. I could see in her eyes that she was ready for some retribution. I knew exactly what that felt like after I saw Bree lose her head. I hadn't expected to have such intense emotions in battle. It was all for real now. I was beginning to see why veterans didn't talk much about the war.

"You've done well, Geena. Plug in and clean up what you can."

Betwi-One, Elysian Front

14

The lieutenant from the Fire Starters came over and pulled me away to join a group of his NCOs. I noticed the LT's name this time, Bekk.

"Switch to command frequency," Bekk said tersely.

I obliged by turning a selector on my wrist controls. I had never been on Command before. It was usually scrambled for the grunts. Bekk's voice was clearer, as if he were standing beside me instead of speaking over a comm.

"Son, it looks like this is it for your platoon. We can't wait any longer for more stragglers. Our ride's on the way down."

I nodded, then replied, "Yes, sir."

"I'm giving you a battlefield promotion. Sergeant Miles, may I have your stripes, please?"

A haggard staff sergeant took off his magnetic metal chevrons and handed them to Bekk. The grizzled veteran didn't look too happy about it but remained silent.

"We don't have any buck sergeants, so this will have to do."

Bekk removed my two metal stripes and replaced them with four. I wanted so badly to salute again but resisted the urge. Bekk shook my hand and let slip a nod of approval. Then his face got serious again, dark eyebrows narrowing.

"Another platoon is on its way down—damn victory squads. You're in charge until they get here, Sergeant. Think you can handle it?"

I replied with a straight face, although inside, I was screaming with joy.

"Yes, sir!"

"Good. This was some kind of bug hive, with many antechambers filled with supplies. Best keep your people out of them. Otherwise, I've declared this area cold. No enemy contacts have been made since you got here. That is all."

I nodded and walked back to my squad to do a head count. There were eight of us left from a whole platoon of forty. I really thought the war was going to be easier. I recalled something Stickman had said during our training, "You'll hear one thing from Command and you'll learn the opposite is true from where you sit on the battlefield. Just trust Command and don't question them."

"They gave you staff sergeant?" Saburo said, noticing my new hardware the minute I walked up.

"It's all they had. I'm in charge until the next platoon gets here. The Fire Starters are moving out. This area has been declared cold. Geena, Selina, and Hutch will pull sentry duty. Everyone else, clean up and recharge your weapons."

Selina spoke up, "What about the MIA's? Someone should try and find any survivors."

I frowned. She was always concerned more about her people than killing the enemy.

"I'll go," Saburo said, standing up.

I looked at my friend for a moment. I wanted to go with him, but now that I was in charge, I couldn't run off with my buddies anymore. I wondered if this was the so-called burden of command.

"Okay, Saburo. But take a partner with you and report back every ten mike."

Saburo tapped Blake's shoulder, and they returned to

where we had come. I sat down at the power cells and plugged in. The newest members of my platoon moved in to meet their new leader. All of them were young, and their nameplates were still clearly readable.

"Some war, eh, Sergeant?" Lane asked. He looked like he was fourteen.

"Not what I expected, that's for sure," I replied.

"Me neither, especially for a Drop and Mop."

Another soldier sat looking forward with a dark expression. "I like it here," he said to nobody.

Everyone turned to look at him, but he didn't react. He just kept staring ahead at the black lava walls. I thought he looked way older than the others. Combat tended to age people, but this guy had only been in the shit for a few hours, the same as the rest of us. I wondered if he was just incredibly focused or else a psychopath.

A scream blasted over the comm lines, startling everyone. I stood up, released my rifle from the charger, and turned around.

"What's happening? Sentries, report!"

Geena was the first to check-in. Fear tinged her throaty voice. "It's not us, Sarge."

"Affirm."

I yanked out my portable scanner and pointed it in the direction that Saburo and Blake had gone. "Saburo, Blake. Report in."

Hearing nothing but static in return, I pointed to the nearest soldier. "Naga, take point. Let's go." Naga armed his rifle and started down the path where Saburo and his buddy had gone.

"What about the other sentries? They're not back yet?" Suz asked, looking back at the power generators and light carts.

Before we could get out of the cavern, the sentries returned. I waved for them to stay at the base camp. I had a last-minute idea: I paired up Naga and Riki and then took Suz with me to form two groups of two. We set out across the lava vein that had split into two tunnels.

Naga flooded the tunnel with his IR spotlight. As far as

we could see, there was nothing but dead bug soldiers and debris. We pressed on.

"Saburo, Blake. Report in."

"I thought this place was cold?" Suz whined.

"Quiet!" I snapped over the comm.

Suz raised an arm, stopping us in our tracks. Then she waved me up. A wounded Elysian soldier lay on the ground a few meters ahead.

"Is it one of them?" I asked, my visor picking an inopportune time to fog up on me. Suz shook her helmet. "No, it's our squad leader."

I crouched a bit and moved forward to help the wounded sergeant while sweeping the area with my hand scanner. "Naga, report."

"Nothing but dead bugs down here, Sarge."

"Okay, cut back and join us."

"Copy."

The other two soldiers returned to the split and came up behind Suz, and I. Suz immediately pulled out her med kit and plugged it into the man's suit.

"Lane, we've found the Second Squad's leader. No sign of our people."

"Copy. All clear back at camp." Her voice sounded further away than she was. Maybe that was just in my head.

"How bad is it?" I asked, looking down at Sergeant Tavers.

"He's low on oh-two and suffering from internal injuries. We have to get him pulled out, or he won't make it," Suz replied, looking up at me.

Call for an evac or wait until the reinforcements arrive? I took a knee and looked into the faceplate of the unconscious man. If I were him, I'd want to be saved at all costs, but that could seriously jeopardize the mission for just one man. My first big command decision was a life-or-death one. It was not what I expected to have to do on my first drop.

I looked at Naga, silently hovering above me.

"Can you drag him back to camp?"

The man nodded slowly as if he disagreed it was the right course of action. But I didn't ask for his opinion, and the man didn't give it.

"Yes."

I turned to Suz, "Go with him. Call for an evac on the sideband when you return to camp."

I stood back as Naga carefully hoisted the wounded man onto his back, and Suz took their rifles. They lumbered back down the tunnel towards camp.

"Riki, this way," I said, heading down the darkened tunnel. It was littered with the corpses of bug soldiers. Their insides had been burned to white ash from Elysian weapons fire.

"Saburo, Blake. Report."

Nothing.

Riki moved over to peer inside an open room. It was darker than the space inside. She flipped on her floodlight and gasped out loud.

"Sarge, I found them."

I came over to Riki, who prevented me from looking inside with a stiff arm.

"They're diced, man. Don't even look."

I eyed her for a moment and then took in the carnage. Both soldiers had been sheared into multiple pieces by high-intensity lasers. The room was empty but there were smoking, short muzzle barrels all over the walls. It was some kind of booby trap. Saburo and Blake must have set it off upon entering the room. It was hard to see my friends like that. They never even had a chance. I fought back tears as I stared hard at the scene. I didn't want to forget the image, as horrible as it was. Finally, I pulled Riki back away from the entrance.

"Lane, we've found them. They're dead. Nobody goes into any storage rooms, understand?"

There was a long pause, and then Lane responded. "Affirmative."

***

I watched the silver evac shuttle lift off carrying the wounded sergeant we had found in the tunnels. Its rockets flowered white as it rose into the black. The sky was clear of flak, unlike when we touched down in the same landing zone.

Nothing but the spray of distant volcanic eruptions mar the view of Betweos dominating the horizon. There was far more beauty here than I ever expected on a battlefield.

My platoon milled around together, getting worked over by armorers from the recently landed Drop and Mop troops. They flooded the area with equipment and personnel, all shiny and new in white and powder blue suits. All I could think of was how easily it would be to take them out with a tactical munition or a few well-placed incendiary rounds. I was starting to think like a soldier all the time now. Everything was a possible ambush point or had a tactical advantage should a fight break out.

A fresh-faced LT came bounding up to me, full of the life and enthusiasm I used to have, not hours before.

"Are you Sergeant Jered?" The man smiled as he spoke, his eyes bright with excitement. I could only stare at him in stunned fascination, unlike how the Fire Starters LT had stared at me.

"Yes, sir."

"Your people are cleared for the next ride back up. Lieutenant Bekk, First Platoon, First Field Army, has requested that your squad be transferred to his unit. First in, last out, eh?"

I didn't react to the news. I just stared off at the surrounding ridgeline behind the man.

"Congratulations! Nobody gets into the First without making a good impression on their leaders. Seems like your squad rescued them from entrapment down there."

I looked back at the man, bewilderment flush on my face.

"Guess you'll be going down with them to the second moon. Good luck, Sergeant. You're going to need it."

The LT patted my shoulder and bounced off to take command of his people. I stared up at the silver clouds of Betweos on the horizon. For the first time in my short career as a soldier, I didn't feel much like fighting.

Betwi-Two, Acheron Front

15

Graul Outpost was the biggest Acheron stronghold on Betwi-Two, a sprawling regolith wasteland of trenches and fortifications protecting an underground bunker that contained the command center. One of the oldest battlegrounds of the war, it was currently owned and defended by the 404th Armored Dragoons, Acheron Army. The dead moon's surface was potted with millions of man-made craters from battles on top of battles. More troopers gave their lives on the dusty gray plains than on any other moon of Betweos. It was a high honor to be chosen to defend it. At least that's what they told us.

It meant absolutely nothing to me.

It was just another barren moon where people died for a government that didn't care about them. All I cared about were my squad mates and myself. Lately, though, I found it to be more and more just myself than anyone else, except for Shen and maybe Slik. But they were in my tribe before they were in my squad, so my loyalty to them exceeded anyone or anything else.

Hacker knew this about me. The Polit Officer ensured I was promoted faster than anyone else so that I would be in charge. The man was more observant than I had given him credit for. He was able to figure out that people followed me regardless of orders. That made me want to distance myself emotionally from nearly everyone. Unfortunately, my job was to care about everyone else when I was in charge. Fucking Hacker.

Alex was no longer in my chain of command. She had been transferred to another ship headed back to Acheron to train a new group of unlucky Toppers. Hacker, however, remained in the Betweos theater and kept an eye on me and my squad. I missed Alex more than anyone else I had met in the army. I felt like she understood me on some level in a way no one else had.

My standard four-armed battle suit with added trench armor was painted regolith gray with dark gray mottling across the top of my torso, upper arms, and back. The helmet's twin oval sensor "eyes" were matte black except where the paint was chipped. Two metal whip antennas sprouted off my shoulders and were snapped onto eyelets on my back. Extra ammunition packs were shoved into racks above my secondary arms. I looked like an armored beetle.

Inside my helmet was a virtual command center of controls and screens that I used my thoughts to navigate. I wasn't thinking about anything in particular, just staring at the gray flats stretching out for kilometers to the small moon's horizon. I couldn't see Betweos from this direction, which faced the coming shadow of the Terminator. Stars beyond the system shined like jewels sprinkled randomly across the black of space. The scene was peaceful and calming. I was supposed to be watching for an expected enemy attack, but that seemed remote and somehow irrelevant compared to the majesty of the universe.

A burst of static over my comms snapped me back to reality.

"Second Squad, run the line," a dispassionate voice uttered.

"Second, copy."

Time to babysit again. I pushed off the ledge I was propped up on and walked down the earthen walls of the trench. Acheron troopers were lined up facing outward, their weapons pointing at the horizon. Waiting. My job was to ensure they were awake and ready to fight.

I didn't need to walk the line to check on them. I could have just looked at their status on my screens, but I preferred to move around rather than stay in one position. Besides, moving helped keep me awake and alert.

The first trooper I came to was Jade. She was smaller than anyone else in the squad but probably the meanest per pound. She constantly reminded anyone who would listen, "Size doesn't matter when you're wearing a battle suit." I had to reach up to tap her right leg. She turned her suit to look down at me.

"You okay?" I asked over suit-to-suit.

"Bring 'em on, sarge," she replied gravelly.

I moved past her to the next person less than a meter away. It was Kate, and she turned around completely to face me as if she wanted to talk. Even inside battle armor, people moved like they have always done. When we looked at another suited trooper, we saw a live image of that trooper's face on our monitors instead of the expressionless, black eyes of the helmet sensors.

"Problem, Kate?"

"My heater is below nominal levels. I'm cold."

Her voice sounded more concerned than she probably wanted to let on. I pulled out a plug from my suit that trailed a wire and stuck it into a socket on the back of Kate's suit. Data started streaming in from her suit's diagnostic program. I read through the logs and sussed out the situation. My armorer had taught me the diagnostic trick, which I was grateful for.

"It's okay for now. We're rotating into view of Suth One; it won't be a problem then."

She gave me a thumbs up and returned to pick up her rifle. I continued down the trench, patting folks on the back and getting their status. Everyone was doing fine, just waiting for something, anything to happen. Waiting was probably the number one fear of any trooper. You waited to go into action, then you waited to see if you would die, and then you waited to get back to the barracks. Once there, you again waited to act on the next duty cycle.

I stopped when I came upon Slik's suit and pulled myself onto the ledge to stand beside my friend. Seeing his face indirectly on the helmet screens was weird, but I could hear Slik's uneven breathing in my earphones and was reassured by his presence.

"Just like back home, waiting for the RUT patrols, huh?" Slik said.

"I wish we had Grim's early warning," I replied.

"No kidding."

After a few minutes of silence, Slik spoke again. His voice was reverent. "Man, I love the stars. I could stare at them for hours."

I slapped my friend's shoulder and climbed back down. "Stay sharp, pal."

Slik huffed and muttered, "Right."

The last two members of my squad were the cannon operators Shen and Prome. Shen was closest to me, wrapped in the clutches of the firing mechanism. Prome sat up higher and more exposed to enemy fire. He was the target acquisition man for the powerful weapon. Fat pipes feeding energy from below snaked up the trench wall between the two troopers. They wore a less armored version of the combat suit.

"You two doing alright down here?"

"Never better," Shen replied.

"Let's get it on. This waiting's terrible," Prome said.

I wanted to say something privately to Shen, but I couldn't do that in the suit. If I did, Prome would hear it. So I held my metal mitten out to her, and she placed hers in a gentle clasp. Every battle was another chance that one or both of us would die. It had become our custom to lock hands for luck. We could see each other's faces through our internal suit cameras. Shen's grainy, red-tinted image looked sad but strong. As I retracted my hand, I started getting a situation report across my screens.

"Standby, I'm getting a SITREP."

When the message finished, I called in my status on the command frequency.

"Squad Two, good to go."

"Copy. Stand to!" came the terse reply.

I started hustling back down the line to get into my position. I switched back to my squad comm channel as I ran. "Enemy dropships have been detected. Condition Red, Attack Imminent. Fire on contact." They already knew what condition we were in. I didn't have to repeat it. But I did anyway.

The moon slowly rotated, causing the darkness to fall away over my head. By the time I got back up on my ledge, I could see the shadow receding across the cratered battlefield. The daylight revealed enemy drop troops as they fell towards the trenches, glittering in the light of the suns. Unlucky bastards.

***

Silvery specks rained down from the sky as if the stars were falling. Flak guns opened up from behind the trenches, illuminating the fading darkness with expanding shards of blue and red. Glittering chaff sprayed out from behind the incoming Elysian soldiers as they fell. Acheron missiles spun awry, chasing the decoys. The carnage was a beautiful and deadly spectacle from the ground. It mesmerized me as my screens produced a lag that slowed the action to the point where it looked surreal.

Red and green bolts of energy pierced the darkness coming from the horizon even before my helmet's sensors could pick out the ghostly bodies of emerging enemy soldiers. Some elements of the Acheron Army began returning fire even before they were able to identify individual targets. During every battle, people would get itchy to shoot something and just open fire without a clear target. My squad were veterans, though; they held their fire until the infrared plumes showed themselves.

All hell broke loose as the battle began in earnest. Explosions lit up the trenches, and equipment and personnel were blown into the airless skies, some of which never returned to the dusty gray battlefield. The second moon wasn't very big, and it was not unusual for debris to get blasted into orbit during the fighting.

The attacking Elysian troops were mowed down by

heavy guns similar to the one Shen and Prome operated. Nobody got close to the lines. It appeared the battle may end sooner than any of us expected. A lull spread across the barren gray flats.

No Elysian soldier reached the barriers erected fifty meters from the trenches. Those barriers would not stop the enemy soldiers from getting through the earthen and metal walls. They were just there to slow them down while Acheron artillery locked onto them and cut them to pieces.

I cycled through the various sensors until I could see the damage clearly. The battlefield was filled with smoldering corpses of blue and white armored enemy soldiers. What a fucking waste. It was like the enemy had more soldiers than sense. I zoomed out my cameras and panned back and forth slowly across the devastation. Body counts started scrolling across my screens. It was less than a hundred dead, and they were scattered before the barriers, none of them close enough to even see with the naked eye. I picked up my rifle and checked the charge. It was still full. I hadn't even fired one shot in anger.

While my attention was averted, the distant horizon erupted in a blinding light as bright as day. The barriers were blown up en masse in a spectacular demonstration of firepower that I'd never witnessed before. I stared in stupefied horror as the enemy poured through the falling debris in a solid wave of blue and white armored suits that swarmed towards the first row of trenches like water from a broken dam.

"Second Squad, stand to!" I hollered into my comms.

***

The second wave of blue armored troops overwhelmed the first row of defensive Acheron positions. It was a slaughter. Close to forty troopers lost their lives in a matter of minutes. The enemy was now just fifty yards away from my trench. My primary mission was to hold my line. I couldn't let the enemy overrun my position and establish a foothold on Betwi-Two.

The troopers in the first trench had failed, and now the enemy had a position from which to launch attacks at Graul

Outpost. It was my job to hold them, and if I couldn't hold them, to die trying.

"Listen up! We have to hold them here. Reinforcements are not coming until tomorrow," I ordered.

I could hear the disgruntled replies from almost every trooper in my squad. Finally, Slik's voice rose above the static. "We ain't going to last that long. They outnumber us and outgun us at this point. Whatever we're going to do, we better do it fast."

There was every reason to believe the enemy would regroup and attack again. I only had a few minutes to get ready. An idea burst into my head like a flare. I jumped off my wall and ran back down to the end of my line, issuing a command while running. "Don't shoot until they get out of the trench. Repeat: don't engage until they charge. Slik, meet me at Shen's position."

I got positive replies from everyone over the inter-suit comms as I got to Shen's position just after Slik. She turned to look at us as I started removing the access panels around her power lines. The lines moved in two directions, backward to the command post and forward to the trench that was just overrun. The access tunnel was smaller than a fully armed trooper and dark as space inside.

"Shen, Prome, get down here. Slik, start taking off your extra armor."

I began taking Slik's armor off. Another trooper named Trent helped me remove more plating. It was obvious to Slik and Shen what I had in mind. Every good trench tribe knew how to fight in metal tunnels. I explained my plan so that we were all on the same page. It came together in my head as I spoke it aloud.

"The tunnels are new since the last attack, so we'll probably catch them off guard," Slik added enthusiastically. I could tell he loved the plan.

"Get me next," I ordered. Trent and Slik both removed my added armor as Shen and Prome joined us at the entrance to the maintenance tunnel.

Prome was a big man, almost a head taller than Shen. He went after myself and Slik, with Shen bringing up the rear.

Shen attached more ammo to her exoskeleton frame and took out her trench rifle.

I switched to the command channel. "Control, this is Two. We need suppression fire in ten mike. Flood the area in grid 240."

There was a quick response from Battle Control. "Copy that, Two."

I turned on my floods, illuminating the dark, narrow tunnel. Then I ducked in a crouch and headed inside. Slik charged his rifle and ducked in after me. Trent handed Prome a couple of extra shock grenades. Prome took them and waved a mock salute back. Then he entered the tunnel with Shen bringing up the rear.

After a long slog through the tunnel, I reached the forward trench access doors and stopped. I turned back to see the others come to a stop behind me. They were shadows in a dark tunnel, backlit by each other's floods. I faced the panel again and scanned the area behind the doors. Two human-shaped IR signatures betrayed enemy positions. I glanced at my chronograph readout and waited patiently for Battle Control's attack.

Right on time, the ground began to shake, and bits of regolith fell from the tunnel's ceiling. I held up my hand for a moment and then dropped it forward. I blasted through the thin metal panels and pushed them into the trench. I moved to my immediate right, and Slik moved left as he exited on my heels. Enemy troops were startled and didn't even return fire in the first few seconds of our attack. I blasted away at anything moving, my secondary arms lobbing concussion grenades as I moved forward.

Prome exited the tunnel and followed Slik, shooting his pulse rifle in a continuous stream of death. Shen exited the tunnel last and followed me, shooting whomever I missed. The firefight was over quickly as the surprise attack killed every Elysian soldier along the trench. Their blue and white armored bodies piled on top of each other in pools of their blood.

The battle was over in less time than it took us to traverse the tunnel. The few surviving Elysian soldiers hopped out of the tunnel and back into the craters where they had come from. They didn't last long there as the artillery rained death down on them. The gray dust of the moon was wet with dark blood. I surveyed the carnage and watched as the others tossed the dead soldiers over the walls of the trench and pulled the only two Acheron casualties aside. We would use the tunnels to get their bodies back to base.

I stood over their silent, armored bodies and removed their data chips. Each person's name scrolls the causes of death. Deeks died from the shock of losing both of his legs at the waist. He only lived for a minute after being hit. Jade was hit in the head and died instantly. Death was often swift if you were lucky.

"It could have been worse," Slik said, standing beside me.

I cleared my screen. "Have the others form up on this row. I'll report in."

"Right."

Slik moved down the trench and I proceeded to undo the comms antenna to send my report. It whipped above my head and waved back and forth in the brilliant light of the two suns.

"Control this is Squad Two."

A scratchy female voice wavered into my ears. "Squad Two, how many kills?"

"Thirty-five enemy kills. Repeat, thirty-five kills."

"Outstanding! How many casualties?"

"Two from my squad. Sending vitals, copy?"

There was a burst of static, and then the air was quiet. I was about to repeat my last transmission when a male voice cut me off. "Squad Two, we're sending up replacements. Your LT was KIA. I'm placing you in charge, Sergeant Major. Prepare to move forward. Copy?"

It was the voice of Captain Karty. I sighed. Promoted again. Damn, bastards.

"Negative copy. Can't you send us a new LT? Over."

"Son, you're it for now. Nice offensive."

"Shit."

"What was that?"

"Copy, Control. Squad Two out."

I switched off the command channel before I caught hell for the slip. I activated my secondary arms and turned them into fists. Then, in anger, I started repeatedly punching the regolith walls of the trench.

I heard Shen's voice over the comm. "They must have promoted him again."

Slik had returned and stood watching my fit of rage. "Heroics always come with a price in the army. Gaven, if you keep this up, you'll either be dead or a general in charge before this ends."

"I'd rather be dead," I uttered as I backed away from the wall and lowered my secondary arms.

All the remaining troopers in my squad were staring at me.

"We're not going back to base. A new squad is joining us, and we're moving forward."

Slik managed to shrug in his light armor and said, "Here we go again."

Betwi-Two, Elysian Front

16

I stood outside momentarily and caught sight of a single Elysian drop ship slipping silently overhead. It launched a fresh platoon of soldiers into the dark skies over Betwi-Two. Fifty shiny metal tubes fell in random streaks. Behind them, the sky became engulfed with the explosion of their drop ship. Nailed by two unwavering missiles launched from Acheron ground forces, the drop ship fell to the moon in millions of glittery pieces just over the horizon. A piece of me died for the brutal loss of Elysian lives.

I never fully realized just how scopious the war effort was until I got to the front. Both sides had dozens of ships and thousands of people working behind the scenes to get soldiers where needed. It was a truly impressive operation. I'll never disrespect a soldier who wasn't in the infantry. If you were at the front, you were just as likely to be killed as any groundpounder.

The war was not as glamorous as the dramas would have you believe. It was a lot of sitting around waiting to do something, followed by moments of sheer terror. Even in the

First Army, First Platoon, the soldiers were just like anyone else when it came to fighting. The only difference I could tell was that they were resigned to it and didn't complain much. They also had an instinct for adapting to change and stress minute-by-minute. Their battle armor wasn't bright blue and white anymore. They'd all been hastily sprayed with gray paint to help them blend in with the regolith. Some of the cleverer soldiers had found ways to mount the heavier enemy armor plates to their suit armor. Anything to increase the odds of their survival was a good thing.

I ducked back down into my command bunker, pulling aside the torn fabric someone had put over the entrance. I stopped at the portable metal table in the middle of the room covered in dusty terrain maps of the battlefield. My maps were hours outdated, and I was impatiently waiting for new ones.

A courier came in and coughed over his com-link. "Message from above, Sarge."

I faced him and saw his startled reaction to my face. My hair had grown out, I hadn't shaved in days, and my eyes were probably still swollen from lack of sleep.

"Report," I snarled.

"The last platoon of noobs just came down. Their drop ship was destroyed."

"I saw that. How many made it?"

"All but a few."

I nodded. "Have the new maps brought to me ASAP. Dismissed."

The courier started to leave and then stopped. "Sarge?"

I gestured for the man to speak but didn't turn around.

"One of the new guys in my squad wants to see you in person. Says he knew you back in the world."

I didn't react; I just stared at the maps on the table. The courier decided to clarify. "He's from one of them Victory Squads. You know, last in, first out type. I'll tell him to shove it," the man said, turning to leave.

"What's his name?" I asked, turning my helmeted head ever so slightly.

"Corporal Hector."

Hector. What the hell are you doing here, old friend? I turned around to face the courier.

"Do you know him, Sarge?"

I nodded inside my helmet. "Bring him down here. Oh, and assemble my leads outside."

The courier bowed slightly. "Yes, Sergeant Major." Then he left the bunker.

***

The sunlight was harsh and bright. My visor darkened as I climbed up a short ladder that led to an optical scope resting on the armor of a dead enemy soldier. I peered through the large electronic viewfinder and swung the scope around to focus on a distant hilltop. After weeks of continuous fighting, the trench lines remained locked in a deadly stalemate.

I jumped down off the ladder and faced a handful of weary NCOs. Each one of them was as tired as I was. "It'll be a week or longer until we're resupplied. How are we doing on food and ammo?"

A First Sergeant stepped forward to give her a report. Her name placard read Maye. All I could see of her was the weathered and worn exterior of her combat armor. There was no discernible difference in the outward appearance of either sex in the armor.

"Three days of food and water, but the ammo's going to run out sooner if we get in a prolonged firefight."

I looked over to the next soldier. Geena, one of the old guards, came to this hell hole the same day as I did. "The west side of their line is the weakest. We could be inside in under an hour," she said. Her voice was filled with confidence born from months of combat experience.

A third NCO re-positioned his rifle to the ready. It was Sergeant Naga, his helmet dented and scratched more than anyone else's. The more shit you took in battle, the more respect the others gave you. Nobody was more respected than Naga.

"I agree."

Naga was a man of few words, but his actions spoke volumes. He was locked and loaded. I removed the rolled-up map from under my arm and opened it to show the area we would strike.

"This image is new, and it's already an hour old. But you can see the objective. We should be able to break through in a few hours. It won't be easy, though. I'll need your best soldiers out front."

Everyone bought into the plan; there were no dissenters. That reflected my leadership and genuine confidence that the job could be accomplished.

"I'm going to need someone to stay behind and make sure the noobs don't shoot us in the back."

I faced Maye, who raised her hand in acknowledgment. "I got it, Sarge. We'll have your back."

"Good. If we get pinned down or overrun, you'll have to hold the line indefinitely."

Maye was slower to respond after that. She looked at the other squad leaders. If they failed to take the ridge, she'd probably get the inevitable counterattack, and all her green soldiers, along with her, would likely perish.

"Understood."

Another courier rushed to my side and handed me a new rolled map. I handed him back the old one and unrolled the new one. My leads all huddled around the map as I pointed to the ridge. The image looked exactly like the last one. The enemy hadn't moved.

"Geena, you and your SAC will cut in here," I pointed to the location with the weakest fortification. "At the same time, Naga and I will slip under this heavy gun and take it out. Understood?"

Helmets bobbed.

I rolled the map, and the group took a step back. "Meet at the western tip in twenty minutes. Dismissed."

As my staff dispersed, I noticed the approach of a clean, blue and white soldier. It was someone new to the moon. Only his boots were covered in gray dust. He stopped before me and stared. The name placard on his chest read Hector, but I didn't need to know who it was. I recognized my old friend's gait as he walked up.

I extended a gloved hand to him, and Hector accepted it.

"I never expected you to be a Sergeant Major so soon,"

Hector said over the suit comm.

"It's good to see you, old friend."

Hector let go of my hand and ducked as enemy fire erupted above our heads. I didn't even flinch. I just reached down and pulled up my friend. Hector looked over my worn armor.

"I was right. You've turned into a battle-hardened veteran on me."

I showed Hector into the command bunker. Inside, I put down the map and picked up a water pouch. I handed the pouch to Hector, who attached it to his helmet and sucked the stale contents with a straw from inside his helmet.

"How are things back in the world?"

"You're family's fine, the crops were having a bumper year when I left."

Our visors had lightened, and we could now see each other's faces. Hector still looked young and innocent to my war-weary eyes. He set the drink pouch down, and the glint in his dark eyes dimmed as he got serious.

"Trille's fucking going out of her mind! Your dispatches stopped coming about a month before I left."

That outburst surprised me, but I couldn't deny my detachment from the old life in Elysia. Home seemed so far away now and so long ago.

"I've been in this hellhole for months. We don't get incoming dispatches until we rotate back to the ships."

Hector slapped the table in anger.

"That's bullshit, Sergeant! You just don't want to talk to her."

My anger began to rise. Who the hell was this guy to lecture me about anything? "Look, I'm going to die here. We're all going to die here. This fucking war is not what we thought it was. It's sheer madness!"

I moved closer to Hector, who backed up as if he half expected a fight.

"The more rank I get, the more I realize how much we were duped into signing up for this shit. It's better for her if she just forgets about me. I'll probably be dead soon, and she can get on with her life. Preferably with someone smart enough not to join the damn army!"

I moved away, pacing the confined room like a caged animal.

"I don't believe what I'm hearing. What happened to the Victors of Betweos?" Hector said. His voice was defeated.

I picked up my rifle and shouldered it. As I brushed past Hector, I said, "One of us grew up."

***

Outside in the trench, the black sky was filled with exploding shells and colored beams of plasma. A battle was raging on a nearby ridgeline. My soldiers were not affected by it. They were preparing to head out on our latest mission, ignoring the chaos. I ducked into another field bunker. It was a communications post named Comm-Fiver. The walls were lined with power generators, portable transceivers, and secure computers. Selina had been transferred to Comm-Fiver a few months back, and her unit had been locked alongside mine for several months.

The bunker was shielded, and it had an airlock. It was one of the few places on the moon where you could risk taking your helmet off. The other is the Processing Bunker buried beneath tons of regolith at Graul. Front-line soldiers cycled back to the PB for much-needed showers and sleep. Even the commanders knew they couldn't expect soldiers to fight indefinitely without periods of calm to reset their nerves.

Selina and I managed to hook up on our downtimes a few months ago and, in the process, started seeing each other romantically. There was no privacy down there, but that didn't stop us. Torrid love-making under covers and in the farthest corners of the showers went a long way towards keeping our sanity during the intense fighting on the surface.

I hadn't thought about Trille or home in a long time. After arriving at Betweos, I stopped sending her dispatches and had hers rerouted to random soldiers, hoping to confuse her enough to stop trying. Those that got through to me I routinely deleted without reading. At some point, I stopped getting them from her and eventually all but forgot about our engagement. The only woman in my life now was the dark-eyed, gray-haired Selina, and I was perfectly okay with that.

I was free and unbound from social constraints when I was with Selina. She indulged my wildest desires, and I returned the courtesy without coaxing. Other soldiers randomly hooked up with partners and then broke off, only to hook up with different ones during the next downtime. But Selina and I stayed together and didn't seem interested in trying out different partners. We had garnered a reputation for being sexual snobs, rebuffing everyone's advances while remaining loyal to each other. When nobody knew if they would live another day, intimacy took on a new level of importance. Nobody wanted to fall in love. They just wanted to feel good for the moment because it might be their last happy moment alive.

The only thing Selina and I spoke about that was not related to the killing above or the sex below was the Bug Myth. I had become immune to her conspiracy theories and dogged belief that the enemy was not bugs but other humans. I tried to argue with her against it but eventually just gave up and tuned her out. It was easier to feign interest than to constantly correct her silly lies and false arguments. After a while, I just let my mind wander whenever she started to rant. Sometimes, I thought about the world I had left behind, and sometimes, I thought about whether I would die the next day or be spared, only to have to wonder about it all again the next day.

Selina was wearing dark gray fatigues, and her hair was pulled into a tail, with loose strands falling into her eyes. I loved her freakishly gray hair. She looked over her shoulder at me, lifting her headphones off her ears. "Hey you, what are you doing here?"

I bent over and snuggled against her exposed ear. "I'm heading out to the western front. Wanted to see you before I left."

She looked confused. I'd never surprised her like this before while we were on duty, which made her uncomfortable. "Okay."

"It's nothing. I'll be back for chow."

Her dark eyes narrowed. "Better get going then."

Looking into her eyes, a sudden thought sobered me out

of my good mood: She's more important to me than I am to her. She didn't seem the least bit concerned for my safety. She looked troubled that I had even stopped by. I swallowed hard and turned to leave.

"Hey, Sarge," she called out after him.

I stopped and slowly turned around to face her. She got up, approached me, and touched my chest plate. "I'm sorry, you just took me off guard coming here. Are you not expecting to return?"

I shook my greasy head of hair and smiled. "It'll be fine. No worries."

Her face softened, melting the chill off my heart. She kissed me and smirked as she returned to her station. I watched her until she sat down, locked my helmet, and left.

Betwi-Two, Graul Outpost

17

Gaul Outpost's rear echelon backed up to a craggy mountain ridge as old as the moon. Tunnels were dug into the mountain, and hollowed-out regions were used for supply depots. After months of fighting on the front lines, my platoon was rotated back to the depot to clean and repair the other trooper's armor. Being the senior ranking member, I was made the depot's Top. The duties didn't get me out of work but put me in charge of several squads of soldiers responsible for maintaining the platoon's armor and weapons. It was cake next to fighting all the time. We were still in a combat zone, and we still had to put down our tools and pick up our rifles whenever called upon.

I was okay with that. Most of my days were spent dealing with repairs to suit armor and managing the limited supplies when there was a lull in the fighting. Not having someone shooting at you all the time did wonders for morale and let you think about other things, like who to knock boots with. Shen and I were out in the open now, and nobody seemed to care. Even Command didn't reprimand anyone screwing whomever they wanted so long as the order was maintained and the repairs got completed promptly. I had no trouble maintaining order and ensuring our jobs were finished correctly. Sometimes, personnel issues came up, and I usually settled them quickly. Once in a while, a couple of the younger troopers would be fighting over the affections of some young thing, and I would have to come between them. A good wall-to-wall counseling usually solved it and left them unwilling to test me on other stuff.

Lately I had noticed that Shen was slipping away somewhere when she was supposed to be on duty. She always had some lame excuse to explain where she'd been, but I never bought them. I had Slik tail her on more than one occasion, and he couldn't find anything incriminating like another man or woman or any other misconduct. Still, it bothered me more than it should have. Am I jealous, or just starting to get too close to her? I wasn't entirely certain anymore. It seemed petty and distracting when I thought about it, but I still hated it when she slipped away unexpectedly.

Slik was convinced Shen was talking to a Polit Officer and reporting on what my squad was doing. But then, Slik was always distrustful of authority to the point of being paranoid. I tended to ignore my friend's suspicions about most things, including what he thought of Shen. After all, if it had been up to Slik, he would have killed Shen back on Acheron.

I looked over at Slik, who was hammering out the dents in a piece of armor across the bay. Sometimes, I wondered if Slik was going behind my back with Shen. It would have been the perfect double cross because I would never have suspected the two of them would ever like each other enough to fuck around. Once, I had Slik tailed to find out where he was when he and Shen went missing. Slik was banging someone all right, but it was not Shen. Slik tended to do things privately and never bragged about his conquests to anyone, so I wasn't even sure the man was interested in such things. Finding out he was horny, after all, made me respect him in ways that killing enemy troops just didn't cover.

I finished and told the trooper to beat it back to the front. Another four-armed trooper approached, bearing the markings of a field-grade officer. It was Captain Karty.

"Sergeant Gaven, we have a weak spot on the western flank. Take some of your people and scope it out. You might have to reinforce it or something."

I stood up and saluted him. You couldn't salute outside in the combat zone for fear of snipers, but it was expected back here in the rear with the gear. Otherwise, you'd catch all kinds of unnecessary crap for not doing it.

"Sir, we're not fitted for combat armor. We haven't been on the line for a month now."

"You're my most experienced fighter. I'm not sending you to the front, just the western interior. Now get the hell over there and tell me what you see."

I saluted again. "Yes, sir."

Karty didn't return the salute; he just turned his back and strode out of the area. I swore at him in my head and then went over and picked up a couple of rifles and some grenades. I strode over to where Slik was finishing his job and handed him one of the fully charged rifles.

"What's up, Top?"

"Karty wants us to check for signs of a breach on the western flank."

Slik stood up and took a weapon from me. "Oh, yeah. Combat. For a while there, I thought we were stuck back here."

"Let's get this over with so we can get back here and relax."

Slik found his helmet, and I helped him secure it. He did the same for me. We could lounge in the depot without our helmets, but we all wore our SBAs. After loading up with grenades, we trudged off down a darkened corridor towards the western flank of the outpost.

Slik and I strolled down a high-ceiling corridor of carved lunar rock. Horizontal grooves in the gray rock only went up a few meters before giving way to the broken rock. Only a few red marker lights illuminated our path along the dusty floor. We carried our rifles loosely since we weren't anticipating using them. I turned on a flood light with my secondary battle arms and pointed it up at the ceiling, looking for any signs of damage.

A battle raged several hundred meters beyond the wall and we could feel the vibrations from heavy enemy shells impacting the mountain. Bits of rock and dust fell on us as we walked.

Slik was a few meters behind me, pointing his flood along the grooved walls. "Looks okay to me, man. Let's get out of here."

I continued forward. "Just a little further."

"Damn, I knew you were going to say that."

We walked a bit slower, sweeping our floods back and forth until we found a pile of freshly crumbled rocks. I pointed my flood to the ceiling and saw the black of space accented with distant stars' cold, unblinking stare.

"This is serious," I said.

"I knew it."

"Stay here, I'm calling it in." I moved away from the fissure and undid my long-range antenna. It sprang open above my helmet, waving back and forth on a spring.

"Command, this is Survey One. We've got a massive fissure open to space down here. Advise shutting down this tunnel, over?"

A burst of static filled my ears as Captain Karty responded. "Alright, Survey One, get your asses back here ASAP!"

"Copy, out."

Slik had been feeling the rough edges of the wall where the fissure had reached the floor. I switched back to the intercom. "Okay, let's roll."

Slik turned around and headed back towards me.

I took two steps before a massive explosion outside caused half the corridor to slide down on top of us. I screamed, "No!" and moved towards where my friend had just stood. A massive pile of rock and debris completely buried Slik.

More rock started falling, forcing me to continue forward using my secondary arms as legs. I hurdled rock and stone, trying to outrun an avalanche. The rock and dirt came down harder as gray lunar dust washed through the tunnel, obscuring my view.

Betwi-Two, Elysian Front

18

I directed incoming rounds onto a reinforced Acheron gun turret on the mountain's western slope. It took a few salvos to hit the mark, and when it did, a massive explosion sent the top of the turret up into the blackness of space and rained down gray rock and dust. Everyone was covered in the dust as we hunkered down.

I raised my head and got to my knees to see better. As the smoke settled, I saw the demolished turret and what looked like an opening into the mountain. I lowered an external device over my visor that magnified the visual. It was a fissure.

I signaled Naga, who was already on his feet ahead of me, to circle around the turret to investigate the fissure. Then I called back into Command to confirm the target was destroyed and prevent them from pummeling the area with more shells.

"Command, Blue Four. We're going to investigate an opening in the mountain behind the turret. Ceasefire, copy? Ceasefire."

There was a burst of static over the comms before a voice responded dejectedly. "Copy, Blue Four. Ceasing fire."

Don't sound so excited about it, Command. I waved to the others in the squad, who were getting to their feet to follow Naga up the side of the mountain. They staked out defensive positions around the fissure as I walked over to the ridge and peered inside. It was dark, but I could see a dim red light not far below.

I looked back at Naga, who shook his head. "Bad idea, Sarge."

I waved him off. It wasn't that far down, and no enemy contacts were on my screen. The hairs on my neck were prickly as I descended the pile of loose rock and regolith. I was breaking the battle buddy rule by going in alone, but I no longer cared about procedures. I just wanted to see what the hell was down there. Did we blast into the back side of the enemy fortress, or was this just an empty hole? The red light indicated to me that there had to be something there.

"Sarge, we're kinda exposed up here," Naga's voice nagged at me.

I ignored him and slid my way down to what looked like a carved floor of a corridor. I hit my flood lamp and panned across the darkness. It was a corridor. We had broken into the enemy fortifications.

"I'm inside the enemy fort, Naga. Signal Command we have a breach and get down here.

"Copy."

I took out my rifle and killed the flood. It was stupid to have turned it on before scanning in IR. I lit the area in IR and watched the mono-color display across my screen. There were no signs of any other life displayed. I let out a long, slow sigh of relief.

The chamber was suddenly lit as bright as day as something shot up from behind a pile of rubble to the crevice where I had entered. The rocket rose on a pillar of flame until it got to the opening and blew up. The resulting explosion caused the fissure to seal itself up as more rock and debris dumped onto the chamber floor. I was quickly buried under the rubble in a cloud of gray dust.

***

The corridor was dark and still. Dust from the regolith above had settled, and the only light was a dim red marker a few dozen meters from the collapse. A narrow white beam flicked on and scanned the rubble with laser-like intensity. It stopped on a frozen enemy figure sitting upright against the far wall.

I raised my rifle and shot out the light with one pull of the trigger. It was answered with a plasma flash from the ugbug's rifle. The shot impacted beside me and took a chunk out of the rock wall. I pulled myself up and dove for protection behind a boulder nearly as big as I was.

I shot off a flare from the back of my suit. It careened off the newly sealed ceiling and shined like an intense star, bathing the whole corridor in harsh, white light. The flare hovered above us as we both tried to take defensive positions.

I saw the enemy bug soldier trying to hide behind a boulder half its size. Its six legs were sprawled out in a pathetic effort to lay low. I drew a bead on the bug and squeezed the trigger. Nothing happened. I twisted the rifle and looked at the charge meter on the weapon's side. Three segmented red zeroes showed on the display. It was empty. I tossed the rifle in the direction of the bug soldier. It clattered on the stone floor halfway between us.

The bug started to move. I watched in fascination as it angled for a better shot at me and then didn't shoot. What the hell? Are you out, too? The bug soldier didn't move. It didn't try to read the gun's charge or switch positions to fire a secondary weapon. It just lay there, pointing its gun at me and not firing.

I wondered if it was being held in position until more bugs arrived for backup. That didn't make much sense, given our current situation. What looked like another recent cave-in blocked the way back into the mountain.

"Take the shot, bugger! What the hell are you waiting for?" I shouted inside my suit. The alien couldn't hear me; even if it could, it probably didn't know my language. I sat back and pondered the situation. I could try approaching the bug soldier and see if I could get the thing to fire at me. Or I could sit tight and wait for Naga to open the fissure and give me some backup. I looked up at the solid rock high above, shielding my eyes from the intense light of the flare. It would shine for another few minutes before dying and falling to the ground.

I decided to force a fight, recalling our No Quarter directive. I stood up and walked across the open ground between us. The bug soldier stood upright, still pointing his rifle at me. I stopped and stood over my empty rifle.

The bug held out his rifle from his side and dropped it to the ground.

"Ah, you were empty," I taunted. "I knew it."

The bug soldier took a few steps toward me, and I withdrew the same amount, keeping the distance between us equal.

"I'm not stupid, bugly. I know you got cannons on your suit."

The heads-up display on my visor started sputtering and then winked off. It wasn't really of any use to me anyhow. The enemy was standing in front of me.

The flare began to flicker above us and started to dim. The bug soldier pointed up, and I followed his gaze. The flare went out and fell to the ground. I shot off another one that emitted a blue-white strobe. It gave our movements a slow-motion look to my now unaided eyes.

I felt the earth move underneath me. More rocks and boulders started to fall. Naga was coming for me. Using the confusion to make a move, I charged the bug soldier. It fired its personal defense cannons but missed me and opened a hole underneath us.

We fell a few meters into a cavernous pit with a metallic floor. Heavy metal doors closed above us, cutting off the flare's light and protecting us from more falling rock and dirt.

***

I opened my eyes and saw myself in a metallic room with flickering, fluorescent lights along the walls. A few meters away, the bug soldier was lying on his back under a smaller rock. My health meters were green, but my head was still ringing from the fall. I slowly got to my feet and noticed my rifle nearby. Picking it up, I re-checked it for a charge. It was still empty. I held onto it anyway, watching the bug for any signs of life.

There didn't seem to be any way out of our room. Smooth metal walls and a rough textured metal floor were impenetrable. What the hell place was this? Something told me the bug didn't know either. Maybe it was just a soldier's intuition. The design didn't look like an Acheron Army one to me. It sure didn't look like anything my side had built, either.

The bug began to stir. It righted itself using its middle arms and stood staring at me with one of its two metallic eyes busted up pretty good. Considering what had happened before, I made sure to stay at least a few steps away from it.

The entomol raised two arms to its head and started to detach the heavy helmet. I rechecked my screens and got no reading on the room's atmosphere. I assumed it was still a vacuum, like on the moon's surface. I doubted the bug would be exposing itself if there were no air of some kind. Perhaps this was part of its base after all.

The large helmet released a cloud of gas as it unlocked. I wondered what toxic air the bug breathed in its home world. I was all too happy to keep my helmet on.

A thought flitted through my head. It was annoying and troublesome, given my current situation. What if it's not a bug? What if Selina was right about the Bug Myth? I bit my lower lip and watched the helmet slide up and off the bug's armored suit.

It was a man! A human being! A young one with an intense stare the equal of any Elysian soldier I had met. The man tossed his heavy helmet to the side, where it made a loud thud on the metal floor. The noise startled me out of my open-mouthed stare.

"What the hell are you looking at?" the man asked.

I couldn't respond. I just stood there. My weapon fell from my hands and clattered on the floor. The sound startled me. After another long moment of watching the sweaty-headed human stare back at me, I removed my helmet and let it fall to the ground.

"You're human?" I stated, still in utter disbelief.

"No shit, what did you think I was?" the man replied.

"You, you were; I mean, we thought we were fighting bugs."

The man looked at me as if what I said was insane.

"Seriously? How can you be that naive?"

I had no response for that. I just shook my head in disbelief. She was right. Selina and her Peacers were right. We were fighting other humans all this time. Un-fucking real.

"But you have six legs," I finally stated.

The human soldier shook his head and approached me. "These secondary arms are mechanical. I only have two arms and two legs, just like you."

Standing before the man, I could smell his body odor and realized he smelled exactly like every other soldier I fought with. Looking closer at the man's unshaven face, I noticed the veins on his temple were dark yellow, not blue like mine. There was a cut across his temple that bled a yellowish substance.

"Why isn't your blood red?"

The man shook his head as if he were talking to a child. "It's the goop the army injects to fortify us for combat. Gives us better oxygen flow than the iron in the blood."

I nodded as if I understood, although I didn't.

"What's your name? Mine's Gaven."

"Jered."

Gaven reached out with his gloved hand to shake my hand. We shook like gentlemen over an agreement. My mind was still reeling from seeing the impossible.

"We speak the same language, too," I said.

"Are all Elysian soldiers as quick as you?" Gaven asked. He moved past me, running his metal-clad hands over the stainless-steel walls.

"What are you looking for?"

"A way out of this place," Gaven said, pointing up with his right lower arm. "It appears that we are trapped in here."

I surveyed the room closer this time. But my eyes kept coming back to Gaven. I still couldn't believe I was fighting other humans. Everything my government had told me was a lie. Everything.

"There has to be a ventilation system in here if we can breathe."

Gaven's spare arm pointed over to the far wall where a narrow slit ran half the length of the room. "Yeah, try and keep up, will ya?"

"I'm looking for a hidden door or something. Help me out here."

I walked to the nearest wall and ran my fingers along it in the same fashion as Gaven. It was perfectly smooth stainless steel with no grooves, indentions, or controls.

We met back where we had started. I was still staring uncomfortably at Gaven. Maybe it was a trick, or maybe Lacithe lured me into a trap, and this was some kind of test.

"Look, stop staring at me, man. I'm human. We're all humans. But I ain't from your world."

My eyes narrowed suspiciously. "What's your world like, anyway?"

Gaven seemed annoyed again with having to explain reality.

"Acheron is a dead planet. The surface is toxic, nothing grows under permanently cloudy skies and acid rain. Civilization moved underground a long time ago. Only surface gangs live outside, where the toxic conditions slowly kill us."

I could tell I might have touched a nerve with the haggard soldier.

"Is that where you came from, the surface?"

Gaven nodded. "The army takes the strongest of us and turns us into soldiers to fight in their war. I was captured and brought here against my will. If I survive my tour, I can live as a lower-class citizen instead of a Topper. What's your excuse?"

I shrugged. "I volunteered to come here. I joined the army to defend my world from the bugs."

Gaven shook his head. "Damn, I don't know which of us was duped better."

He moved to a wall with some cryptic writing on it. "Can you read this?"

I followed him over and studied the words. "This is the

ancient tongue of my great-grandmother's day."

Gaven stared blankly back at me. "Can you read it?"

"Air changer pass. I think," I mumbled.

Gaven waited patiently as I fought to read the placard.

"Oh, exit. I think it means exit here."

Gaven looked back at the seamless wall. "How? There's no controls and no opening."

I reached out and touched the placard. "Push here."

A panel about the size of a human sunk into the wall; we grinned amusingly at each other. Then Gaven pushed the button again, and the panel withdrew into a hidden passage. He brought up his weapon, remembered it was empty, and tossed it behind us. He turned on his floods and headed into the darkness.

My light was on my helmet so I just followed Gaven inside with a final look back at the empty main room. As if to fixate in my mind how to get back there. Even if we did come back, there was no guarantee we would be able to get back to the surface.

Betwi-Two, Betweener Station

19

Inside the antechamber, there were more placards. I studied them for a few minutes and then surmised what they were. "It's an elevator, and it only goes down."

Gaven shrugged. "I got no pressing desire to return to the war, do you?"

I shook my head. I was beginning to like this guy. I took a stab at the controls, and the door slid shut behind us. We started to fall.

"I picked the lowest floor," I said.

"Good. Maybe we'll see who's home. Did your people make this place?"

I shook my head. "Not in my lifetime. We were never told about it anyway."

The lift came to a halt, and the door slid open. Both of us stared at the opening. Gaven moved out first, and I followed him closely. It was a control room that hadn't been used in a long time. All the consoles were dormant and covered in layers of fine gray dust. There was a white flag on one of the walls. I moved over to study it. The flag had three circles - red, gray, and blue. I recognized it immediately. It was the symbol of the Bug Myth-believing anti-war Peacers.

"You know this flag?" Gaven asked.

"It's a Peacer Flag. There's an anti-war movement on my planet, and this is their symbol, three circles on a white background."

Gaven and I locked eyes for a moment. Then Gaven looked back at the flag.

"It looks familiar to me. What do you suppose the circles represent?"

I pointed at the circles from left to right, reciting Selina's words: "Blue is my world, gray is Betweos, and red is your world."

"That implies some kind of cooperation, doesn't it?"

I turned back to Gaven with a confused look on my face.

"I don't understand. What are you suggesting?'

Gaven shrugged and moved away. "Whoever worked here left a long time ago. These terminals are hundreds of years old," he said, fingering the dust on the control panels.

"Everything in here is old."

I wiped the dust from a stack of papers and tried to read the charts printed on them. "This is a transport schedule. I think this place might have been a shipping station."

Gaven fiddled with the controls and some of the desktop equipment. "This stuff looks like the junk we have on the surface of Acheron. I've never seen it looking so new before."

I moved to another stack of paper and blew the fine dust from it. I picked it up and pushed my finger across the page, trying to read the ancient words.

"This language is very archaic. I think it's Ellenico, the old tongue."

I read something, and my face scrunched up in thought. "This is something called a Betweener Station."

Gaven stared blankly back at me. It clearly meant nothing to him either.

"Apparently, they were traders. Facilitating trade between Elysia and Acheron hundreds of years ago."

Gaven came back over to look at the pages I handed

over to him as I read them. He glanced at them briefly and set them down on the desk, still unable to read them. I read on, slowly beginning to piece together what was going on.

"Here's orders for tons of corn, soybeans, and meat, all coming from Elysia and heading towards your world. Here's a return shipment from Acheron to my world for electronics and machined goods."

Gaven studied the charts closer because he could at least make sense of pictures and graphs. I moved around the control room and felt air blowing from the vents above them. A few panel lights lit up as if waking from a deep sleep. I marveled at what kind of power source could survive for so long.

"I think we woke this place up by coming in here. Can you hear the air exchangers? I can feel the deck vibrating. I wonder what kind of power they used that could survive unattended for so long?" I asked.

Gaven lingered behind me, his voice a suggestive whisper. "Maybe this place was never abandoned?"

Along the far wall were panel windows or displays of some kind. I moved over to them and touched them with my gloved hand. The glass-like material was smooth but opaque.

The instrument panel below me lit up. Old screens started glowing, and keyboards formed on the panels. The overhead lights winked on, causing both of us to look up.

We waited for something else to happen, but nothing did. Fresh air circulated in the room, and screens came alive, showing text-based terminals with scrolling data. I found more documentation and read it carefully to understand it.

"I don't see any evidence this was a military facility. Do you?" Gaven asked.

I shook my head slowly as I read something pertinent. "This is a trade manifest for transfer ships. It looks like the Betweeners stayed here while Betweos orbited our home stars. That's like a decade or more. When the planet orbited Elysia's star, food and raw metals were transferred to this moon and stored. When Betweos shifted back around your home star, the goods were transferred to Acheron, and in return, finished products were shipped back to Betwi-Two bound for Elysia."

Gaven moved to the dust-covered glass screens and used a finger to draw out a diagram of the binary star system in which they both lived. Acheron orbited a small, red dwarf star named Kolasi; he drew it out and labeled it. Then he drew the yellow star known as Paradis and the blue-green world of Elysia. Standing back for a moment to surmise the drawing, he traced the orbit of Betweos in a lopsided figure eight around both stars. When the planet came around Paradis, it was close enough to be reached by rockets launched from Elysia easily. When it swung around Kolasi it was equally near enough for people living on Acheron to reach.

"So, Betweos was a stepping stone. A convenient way to move people and goods from one planet to another," Gaven stated.

I studied the drawing and nodded. "It must have started a long time ago. We've been taught that all life evolved on Elysia over the millennia."

Gaven shook his head and pressed, "No, don't you see? We evolved on Acheron. Our star, Kolasi, is far older. It must have captured Paradis at some point. Who knows where the planets originated."

I was confused. "If that's true, everything I've been taught in school is wrong. I'm stunned."

Gaven started speaking in a respectful tone. "Legends of my people say that long ago, they had used up all the natural resources of their home world and turned it into an unlivable wasteland. The best and brightest people were sent to paradise to start again with a new, unspoiled planet."

"Paradis."

Gaven nodded. "Elysia is an ancient Acheron word for paradise."

"Over the years, Acheron traded with Elysia until Paradise became self-sufficient. The right to come to heaven is what I'm supposed to be fighting for, not the chance to live in the interior of a dead world. I never believed all that crap because I came from the highest, poorest level of society. My chances of ever getting out were next to nothing."

I raised an eyebrow. "And now you could die here," I indicated the moon we were on, "halfway to heaven."

"You'll die here too, halfway to hell," Gaven replied.

I adopted the same respectful tone of his voice. "There are prophecies on my world, too—tales about the dead returning from hell to reclaim our planet for themselves. Of course, the government told us it was a vicious colony of sentient bugs. I never paid those old tales of the dead any attention, largely because they were considered blasphemous.

"Peacer propaganda all speak of us originally coming from Acheron and that we've been fighting other humans all this time, not bugs. Nobody in their right mind took them seriously."

Gaven drew the three-circle Peacer flag on the dusty glass and then turned to face me. "Do you believe the Peacers now?"

I stared at Gaven. It was hard to deny anymore, especially with a human being standing before me in Acheron battle armor. Finally, I nodded. "Yes."

Gaven pointed to the three circles he had just drawn on the glass. "I know where I've seen this before. On Acheron, this is a corporate symbol. It's stamped on everything from gun parts to food containers." He wrote the letters S, V, and K inside each circle. Stratos, Viomichania, Kyvernisi.

I nodded. "In the old language that reads Military, Industry, and Government."

Gaven moved back to the flag on the wall and shook the thick layer of dust off it. Written inside each circle was a light gray letter—S V K. He looked back at me, staring at the flag in disbelief. I saw it for the first time for what it really was.

Gaven reached up to the chest plate of his armor with a mechanical second arm and unscrewed one of the Personal Defense Cannons. He handed me the short barrel. I held it up to examine it. The letters S V K were stamped on it.

I picked up my rifle and set it down on the nearest console. I field-striped it and then showed it to Gaven. The letters S V K were stamped in the blued barrel.

I pulled out a food package from my leg pouch. It was a

blue and gold metallic foil bag with some writing near the bottom. I read it aloud, "SVK Foods. That's the name of the parent company who owns the farm consortium I used to work on."

"I don't think the planetary governments even know what is going on," Gaven said.

I looked back at the charts and flung the papers I was holding. They flew around and down to the metal floor. "There's no mention of any war between our worlds. Why are we fighting now?"

Gaven shrugged as best as he could inside his suit. "Maybe the Elysians didn't need us anymore. Maybe they wanted their independence."

I didn't want to hear that. I looked away in thought. "Why make up the whole Bug story? I don't get the reason for all that subterfuge and death."

"Maybe they knew they would never be able to get you to fight unless you felt threatened. Everybody hates bugs."

"But we would have eventually caught on, right? I mean, all it took to discover the truth was for you to take off your helmet."

Gaven raised his chin. "The Elysians never take prisoners. You kill even the wounded. That freaks us the hell out and leads to higher mortality rates in combat than for your side."

"We're told you don't take prisoners either. Don't your soldiers kill the wounded?"

Gaven shook his head. "Nope. They are taken back to Acheron and reprogrammed. Many of the sons-of-bitches are now our military leaders."

My eyes rolled. How fucking twisted is this war? It keeps getting crazier and crazier the more I learn about it. The war had turned into a funhouse mirror, reflecting a bizarre truth that kept turning my worldview upside down. I looked at Gaven again. The man was unshaven, and his skin was sweaty and dirty from living in a suit for weeks. He was not a bug, and I felt no hatred for him. If I had to shoot Gaven right now, I didn't think I would have been able to pull the trigger.

He was no longer a less-than-human bug that had to be exterminated at all costs. He was just a man, not unlike myself. Gaven was right. I would not have volunteered if I had known that I was going off to war to fight other humans. I might have avoided it at all costs, as most Peacers did.

The realization that I had killed dozens of Acheron soldiers since I had arrived here started to turn my stomach. Some of them might have been my Elysian brothers in arms. I'm a goddamn murderer, not a war hero. Feeling upset to the point of being sick I moved away and sat down with my back to the wall. I felt defeated. "I had no idea any of this was going on."

Gaven picked up one of the old shipping charts and blew the dust off it. It clearly showed orbital paths from Acheron to Betweos at different times when the gas giant's orbit was closer to Acheron. Following the paths with a finger, he said, "Some of these were for incoming shipments, and others were for outgoing shipments. It was all according to some larger plan. The two sides seemed to rely on each other, tied together for mutual benefit. The war must have started after this base was shut down. Dates here indicate that it was close to two hundred years ago. Do you still think our governments are in contact?"

I was barely listening to him. I just stared ahead, not saying anything. Gaven walked over to me and handed me the chart. I took it and listened this time when he repeated the question.

I studied the orbits and compared them to what was happening now. Since the war started, we only fought when Betweos was between our stars. That period lasted about six months before the gas giant system moved out of reach for one side or the other. Because Elysia's star was larger, Betweos lingered longer in the Paradis system than the Kolasi system. I knew these were the decades when there was no fighting, and society seemed to gear itself up for the next time the planet neared the halfway mark. Children had just enough time to grow old enough to join the army.

Munitions plants stepped up output, and farms began filling food stores to feed the troops heading off to fight.

Growing up on a farm, I was well aware of these cycles. Recalling them now, I realized they corresponded to generations. My grandfather fought two campaigns ago; my father was on the transfer ships during the last campaign. I always knew that when I turned eighteen, I would be of age for the next big attack on the moons of Betweos. There was no memory of the war before my grandfather. Maybe Grandfather Jarna was the first generation to fight. This was damn convenient for the government because nobody was alive now who remembered a time before the war.

"There's no evidence that my people know what's going on. We all think Acheron is filled with Entos, sentient bugs bent on our mutual destruction. It's been that way since my grandfather's time. That must have been some kind of a cover-up to have lasted this long."

Gaven sat across from me, using his mechanical arms to ease himself down. "There has to be someone on your side that knows the truth. For us, the Political officers run things, not the military leaders. They all report back to the central government."

My eyes grew larger. "We have them too. They're assigned to every military unit. Do you think they are the only ones that know about this?"

Gaven shrugged. His dark eyes looked away as a thought occurred to him. I saw the awareness. "What? What are you thinking?"

"What if the Polit Officers on my side are Elysian officers?"

I put my hands to my forehead and slowly shook my head. I couldn't take much more of this mind fuck.

"What better way to ensure the deception continues on both sides?"

"I can't believe Stickman is an operative. He seemed like the ultimate warrior to me. Calm and collected and all-knowing." I dropped my hands and looked at Gaven.

"My Polit Officer is Hacker. He does everything he can to piss us off and make us want to hate your side. He slaughtered my trench tribe and told us it was an Elysian missile attack."

"But, we have no such missiles."

"No shit," Gaven said.

"Man, what a hellish world you come from."

Gaven touched his breastplate. "Me? What about you? Your people have convinced the entire planet you're fighting giant cockroaches."

I shook my head slowly, acknowledging the touché.

"I don't think the governments of our planets are running this war," Gaven stated.

I looked over at him. The enemy soldier was stone-cold cold serious.

"Who is then?"

"I think it's the corporation - SVK. They make everything this war uses except the people who die fighting it."

I nodded slowly in agreement. It was true. If SVK were a multi-planet corporate entity, they would have every reason to ensure the war continues. "If SVK were running the war, they would be making untold amounts of profit. Which would be a clear motivation to continue the conflict," Jared said.

"What do you suppose they are doing with all that money?"

I sat my head back against the wall and tried to recall who the richest people in Elysian society were. It wasn't the working class—I knew that for sure—so that left government and business owners. The most wealth seemed to come from agricultural conglomerates and technology companies. They must all be tied into the government and thus into the military.

"My whole society is driven by the cycles of this war, which in turn are driven by the orbit of Betweos. When the planet is in orbit of our star, we work furiously to fortify the moons and stockpile them with munitions and food. When Betweos starts heading back towards your star, we send our troops there to fight. By the time it comes back, we are sending more troops to fight and retake it from your side. In that downtime, we are making babies, food, and weapons.

"The war keeps our economy rising at incredible rates. Since the war started, we've become a more prosperous and healthy society. There is no sickness and no unemployment to speak of. People willingly go off to fight; when they come back, they start families, and when their kids mature, they go off to fight."

Gaven frowned. "The same rhythmic cycle affects my world. But the rich live deep inside the planet, and they regularly raid the surface for the poor wretches who are forced to live in poverty there. The only time the rich come to the surface is to launch missions to Betweos to fight the war. Although, I've heard rumors that there are facilities on the far side of Acheron where supplies are taken from Betweos and distributed to the lower classes."

"I'll bet those supplies are what's feeding your elites. Do you even have agriculture in your world?"

Gaven shook his head slowly. "Not that I'm aware of. But I've never been to the lowest levels."

I got up and went to the screens where Gaven drew his map of the system. I looked down at the controls and started pushing buttons. One of them activated the screens and turned them transparent.

There was a vast room under us with thousands of containers all stacked neatly into rows. I punched more buttons, and lights winked on in the cavernous warehouse.

"Gaven, look at this."

Gaven used his secondary arms to hoist himself and moved to the windows. His mouth fell open in amazement at how large the warehouse was. I had already moved aside to locate another seemingly hidden door. I found the controls and opened them. Air hissed inside from the warehouse.

The door slid aside,, revealing a catwalk that snaked down the side of the warehouse wall to the grated floor hundreds of feet below. I motioned to Gaven before heading down the narrow yellow staircase. Gaven followed but hesitated when he saw how high up we were.

"Come on, what are you waiting for?" I asked.

"I've never been this high up before. I... I don't think I like it."

I waved to him like it was nothing. "Just don't look down, you'll be fine."

Gaven slowly turned to face the narrow catwalk leading to the stairway. He proceeded at a much slower pace than me. It took us several minutes to climb down to floor level. At one point, we were as high as the storage containers stacked three deep.

I started trying to read the labels on the containers. I ran my finger across the ancient language, and my lips silently formed the words I was reading.

"This one's full of seeds. Corn, I think. Huh. That one over there is full of copper."

Gaven came over after reaching the ground and looking much relieved. "Copper is used to make shell casings and tubing for our rifles, among other industrial uses."

I had moved on to another row. "These are full of uniforms. I'm dying to open it and see which side."

Gaven used his mechanical hands to grasp the giant levers to pry open the metal doors. After struggling momentarily to get leverage, he readily opened the container with the uniforms.

When I turned on my torso suit light, thousands of neatly stacked Elysian blue uniforms stared back at us. The style was not current.

"These are old. They were worn by my side when my grandfather served."

Gaven moved on to another row and didn't wait for a translation. He pried open the door and activated his suit lights. Hundreds of stacked rifle cases filled the container. He used his secondary arms to pull one of them free. The SVK Arms label was etched into the aluminum case. Gaven held the case with his secondary arms and opened it with his hands.

They were pristine Acheron army rifles. He found a power pack and slid it into the rifle. The meter on it indicated a full charge.

When I walked up beside him, he handed me the rifle.

"It's an old PR-14 rifle. Rugged and accurate. A damn antique, yet it can still be activated."

I studied the weapon with an experienced soldier's eye. I pointed it at a nearby container and squeezed off a round. The weapon discharged a bolt of plasma into the heavy metal container, leaving a hole the size of someone's head. I looked back at Gaven and smiled approvingly.

"I like it," I said as I examined the weapon closer.

Gaven removed a second plasma rifle. He put a power pack into the weapon and charged it. I looked up and realized Gaven's rifle was pointing at me. I stared at the barrel and then at Gaven. Gaven's lips curled in a grin. Is he going to kill me, I wondered. I suddenly wasn't so sure as I slowly eased my gun barrel in Gaven's direction.

Gaven's grin faded, and I figured it was game over.

Then he swung the barrel of his rifle away as he shouldered it using the cloth strap.

"Wonder what else we can find in here?" he asked.

I slowly shouldered my rifle and looked around. "I'm not sure why such an old facility still has power and breathable air. Makes me think they're still in business."

Gaven motioned the way forward with a secondary arm. "Let's go for a walk then."

Betwi-Two, Betweener Station

20

I took the lead, holding my ancient rifle as if clearing a trench. Jered followed me, covering our six. We worked together as if we were on the same team and not opposing soldiers. It felt strange but not wrong. The main storage room we were in ended in a solid wall that we followed for a while until we could find one of the hidden doors. Before opening the door, Jered touched my shoulder armor.

"Wait. If the next area is occupied, we need to keep our eyes open and be ready to retreat."

I agreed and readied myself for a firefight. Then I opened the hatch, and the door popped open. The area inside was another storage room, but it was well lit, and we heard the sounds of heavy equipment moving around behind the newer-looking storage bins. It was active.

I pointed the way ahead, and we proceeded with caution. There didn't seem to be any alarms to announce our presence despite the fact that the entire facility was unknown to anyone fighting on the surface.

I indicated to slow with a hand gesture as I peered around the edge of a container. Jered waited for me to duck back around. Then he approached so that I could speak without raising my voice.

"There are two individuals ahead, moving what I think are munitions into a cargo carrier," I said.

Jered nodded and then switched positions with me to see for himself. They were several dozen meters away, and their backs were turned to us, so we couldn't really see their faces. Their black uniforms had the now familiar three-circle stencil on the back. The uniforms didn't look especially military; they looked more like worker overalls. They had lower back protection pads for heavy lifting and additional padding on their knees and elbows.

"They don't look military to me," Jered said, turning around.

I don't know why I thought to record at this time. I guess I wanted proof that what we were seeing was real.

"I think we need to record this. Do you have a camera on your suit? All of mine are back on my helmet," I asked.

Jered nodded. He had a single-lens recorder on his right shoulder, which he could monitor with a screen on his inner arm band. He quickly activated the recorder and edged back around to record the workers. They were finishing up and seemed ready to close their container. He only got a few seconds of footage before ducking back.

"We need to get up on one of these containers where I can look down on them."

I pointed to the side of the nearest container. It had footholds and a railing to grab onto. My suit was too big to climb without making undue noise and attracting attention.

"I'll go up and see if I can cross over to where they are," Jared said, starting to climb.

"I'll cover you. Come back down as soon as you get something interesting. Don't linger up there."

Jared waved back to me as he slung his rifle over his shoulder and easily climbed up the container's side.

***

I low crawled across the top of the storage container until I reached the edge that faced out into the open space where the two workers had gone. More forklifts were scattered around and a dozen or so workers, most of whom were loading what looked like an Acheron personnel carrier. I switched on the camera and carefully panned around to take in the whole area. At the far side was an Elysian armored supply vehicle. It was pretty beat up from battle damage and didn't appear serviceable.

Not only was this place active, but vehicles from both sides were in the same building. It was not solid evidence of collusion, but it sure didn't look right. I switched off the recorder and backed away so as not to attract attention. Looking up and around, I tried to locate cameras that would give me away. The walls of the facility were smooth and featureless. Light came from panels above that were flush to the ceiling.

There was what looked to me like a large entrance to the right, big enough to accommodate cargo containers. I watched the workers for a while, trying to see if the door would open and let the Acheron transport through. They all seemed to be just standing around waiting for something to happen. I knew the feeling.

I considered returning to report to Gaven when suddenly, the large entrance started opening. The transporter moved through it and disappeared. Another transporter came inside, this one empty. I recognized its design as being from the Elysian Army. A new container on the far side of the room was opened and workers removed large boxes that I immediately identified as battle suit storage containers. Each one had all the parts needed for a single soldier's suit.

I turned on my recorder and tried to zoom in on the boxes. The camera wasn't designed for long-range recording, and I couldn't get as close as I wanted without losing clarity. The workers loaded ten of the boxes onto the transporter, and then it, too, scooted through the entrance.

I turned off my recorder and backed away from the edge again. I had seen about all I could get from this location. I looked around for a way to get closer and then opted to head back to Gaven's location. My mind was still reeling from the fact that he was a human, no older than me. Coupled with what I had just seen, I despised the war and everyone behind it even more than ever before.

Peering over the edge of the container, I didn't see Gaven below. Shit. Where the hell did he go? There was a scuffling of boots, and I watched two workers walk down the row, heading back to the open area where the transporters were. Where the hell did they come from? I waited until they were gone and then climbed back down to the floor, raising my rifle just in case I encountered more of the black-clad workers.

A noise from behind me caused me to spin around quickly, pointing my rifle. It was Gaven, standing there, pointing his rifle back at me. I lowered my rifle and approached. His voice was just above a whisper. "I had to hide from those workers. Did you see anything up there?"

I nodded. "Yeah, they are supplying both sides of the conflict."

Gaven smiled grimly. "Did you record it?"

I nodded. "We have to get out of here before..." I stopped talking as two workers appeared on either side of us. They looked more startled than us. I could see they were human and they were no older than Gaven and myself.

"Hey, how did you two get in here?" one of them asked.

Gaven and I exchanged looks, and then both of us instinctively flipped our rifles and knocked both men unconscious with our rifle butts. The workers fell without even lifting an arm to defend themselves. Gaven handed me extra power clips that worked in both of our rifles. We didn't stand around waiting for more people to show up. We bolted back the way we had come.

Out of breath after reaching the top of the staircase, I looked back down over the dark warehouse for any signs we were being pursued. The vast room was empty and silent.

"We don't have much time. It won't take them long to discover where we came from," I offered.

Gaven returned to the control room with his rifle ready, half expecting more workers or even Elysian troops to greet us. We were relieved to find the room was empty. The same instruments were lit up as when we left, near as I could tell when I came through the door and closed it behind us. Maybe nobody would ever know we were there. I turned to face Gaven, staring at the map he had drawn on the windows.

"Before I wipe this, you should record me. You know, telling your people we're not bugs or something," Gaven said.

I nodded slowly and motioned for my newfound friend to stand before the windows as I lined up the shot. He had to calm himself after the climb and the run back. As Gaven collected his thoughts, I noticed my reflection in the glass behind Gaven. Perfect.

"You ready?" I asked.

Gaven's combat stare returned as he replied, "Ready."

I pushed record and held my shoulder steady as Gaven recounted where he came from and his long, strange trip to the war. As I listened, I knew he was actively committing treason in the eyes of his people. I didn't know if this would convince anyone of what the two of us had discovered. All I knew was that if I had seen this footage I would be inclined to believe what Gaven said. His sincerity showed a deep sense of kinship, and I felt empathy for what he had gone through.

I suggested he remove his torso piece and try to prove that the extra arms were mechanical. On the outside, they looked for all the world like real, armored appendages. Once he took them off, though, it was apparent they were mechanical. Gaven directed both mechanical arms down to make a temporary stand, then quickly removed his chest piece and his waist piece and stepped out of the suit.

I was amazed at the engineering brilliance of the design. It was clear that the Acheron designers were infinitely more advanced than the engineers on Elysia. I reached out with my suited arm and shook Gaven's hand. Somehow, it was important to note that neither of us hated the other, especially after what we had discovered.

"I'll get some shots of these charts while you suit back up," I said.

Gaven agreed, carefully putting himself back into the secondary arms and sealing himself up. The wall monitors that looked down to the dark storage area morphed into clear windows behind Gaven. I looked up in time to see several more dark-dressed people coming up the staircase. I picked up my rifle and motioned for Gaven to turn around.

The new men were not workers. They wore security uniforms and were armed with weapons unfamiliar to me.

"Open fire," Gaven said as he blasted the walls.

Gaven unloaded and took out three security guards along with most of the wall and maps he had drawn. I had not fired my weapon. They were humans. I was done killing my own kind.

Gaven moved carefully to the smoldering edge and peered down. There didn't appear to be anyone else coming. "We must have tripped an alarm after all."

"Let's go. We have to get back up and get out of here," I said.

We squeezed back into the lift and punched the nearly hidden controls to raise them back to the main floor. The lift opened, and each of us went to his helmet. When I saw Gaven stop before putting his bug-eyed helmet on, I held off donning my helmet.

"Jared. It was a pleasure meeting you. But I hope we never meet again."

I held out my hand again, and we shook.

"I won't fight you if we do meet. Hell, I don't think I can fight at all anymore."

Gaven seemed to understand, even if he didn't quite believe me. "You have to get that recording back to your people, to those who believe the war is a lie."

I grinned confidently. "I'll make sure someone gets it back to Elysia. Don't worry. What are you going to do?"

Gaven shrugged. "I'll think of something. There's someone I've been meaning to settle a score with."

"That Polit Officer who murdered your tribe?"

Gaven nodded grimly. We stared at each other one last time. Eye to eye, human to human. Finally, we both put on our helmets and secured them.

The lift started to cycle again and its doors began to open. We drew our ancient rifles and blasted the lift, emptying our clips and turning it into a smoldering wall of slag.

We changed clips and then looked up. The door that had dropped us into this room was still closed. Gaven and I both aimed at us and blasted away again. One of the sides melted away under the intense heat, leaving an opening large enough for us to climb through above the far wall. Gaven motioned me to climb up on top of his burly mechanical shoulders to reach the ceiling.

I easily pulled myself clear of the room and then surveyed the closed-off tunnel where we had first met. It was still dark and empty. I poked my helmet back into the hole and saw Gaven using his mechanical arms to punch holes in the side of the wall to climb up. In no time, we were both standing in the darkened tunnel.

Gaven found a boulder and used his mechanical arms to roll it over the hole in the fake floor. We both stepped back and reloaded again for the last time. Taking aim above the bolder, we unloaded on the rock wall, and it collapsed over the hidden room. A tiny glimmer of light flared out of the gray wall. I started hearing voices over my comm. I knew my squad mates were looking for me.

I pointed to the opposite wall where it looked like we could blast through to the outside. Gaven waved that he understood, and again, we combined our firepower to blow out an exit for me that led outside.

I slid the power clip from my rifle and handed it to Gaven. It would do me no use on my side and rendered my ancient Acheron rifle inert. Gaven took the ammo and clipped it onto his suit.

I slung the rifle over my shoulder and started climbing. Gaven watched me while watching the opening that led back to the base. When it was clear I would make it out, I turned to look back at Gaven. The bug-suited man was already breaking apart the wall, trying to reach his comrades-in-arms inside the outpost.

I wanted to wave back at him but realized it was dangerous to stick around. I pulled myself out of the rocky tunnel and into the darkness that was the night side of Betwi-

Two. The battlefield was quiet. There was no shelling, no gunfire lighting up the night. It felt like the war was over. In a way, it was.

Betwi-Two, Elysian Front

21

I slid into a trench unannounced and startled a few soldiers milling about outside a bunker. They drew their rifles on me too late to have taken me out.

"Sergeant! We thought you were dead," one of them uttered on the suit's comm.

"Not yet. Where are the Victory Squads?"

The second soldier raised his weary arm and pointed down the trench. In the distance, I saw a transport idling its rockets in preparation for a sprint to orbit. I figured Hector was aboard. Good riddance.

"Gimme some ammo. I'm out," I said, holding up my empty rifle.

The first soldier shoved one of his ammo packs into my waiting hand. He noticed the enemy rifle and said, "Hey, where did you find that old thing?"

I ignored the man and hustled down the trench, still carrying my enemy rifle over my shoulder. I turned to the entrance of Comm-Fiver.

Selina was standing at the far side of the room when I

cycled through the airlock. Her helmet was off, and she froze, staring timidly at me as if she couldn't tell who I was. I reached up and unsealed my helmet to take it off. A relieved smile played across her face. We hugged tightly for a long moment.

"I thought you were dead, soldier," she whispered into my ear. Her breathy voice sent a chill down my spine.

"We have to talk after we return to orbit."

***

The *Elpida* was parked in a stationary orbit around the silvery gas giant of Betweos itself. A thick, cylindrical starship snuggled up against the sleek troop transfer, refueling lines extended and pumped in the gases needed to blast it back to Elysia. Tanker ships like the Káfsima endlessly circled Betweos, dipping low into the clouds to capture hydrogen to fuel the inner-planetary starships, its crew tirelessly evading enemy contact while living in a giant hydrogen sack. I spent much of my free time in space just staring out any available window, marveling at such sites.

Our unit had been rotated back aboard the *Elpida*. I still hadn't spoken to Selina about what I had done while separated from my unit. I lied to Lacithe during my debriefing, telling the Morale Officer that I had gotten stuck inside the enemy fort and could not blast my way out until the enemy had started boring their way through the collapsed rock toward me. Lacithe didn't seem to care much about the incident. I didn't mention finding the older rifle and wasn't asked about it.

I asked him once if anyone had ever gotten trapped inside the enemy fortress. Lacithe shook his head and grunted. I took that to mean that he wasn't interested in discussing the matter. A part of me wanted Lacithe to act suspicious, as if he knew that there might be more to tell about my adventure, but the man seemed bored with the debriefing, and I didn't press the matter. It was clear that he knew nothing of the secret base below.

***

Later, I found my mentor and battle trainer alone in his office. Stickman was preparing his uniform for the next duty day. He let me in, and for the first time, I felt like I was being treated as an equal. Two combat veterans were talking, each respecting the other's accomplishments.

"Sarge?"

Stickman raised his eyes. "What's on your mind, soldier?"

"How many bugs have you killed?"

Stickman's dark face was shadowed, making him appear blacker than space. The whites of his eyes were steady and bright.

"Dozens, maybe more. I've been here longer than anyone else. My body count is hard to beat."

I nodded in agreement. "Sure is, sir."

Stickman looked at me as if he sensed something was wrong. I wanted to tell him about what happened with Gaven but knew I couldn't. The older soldier studied me for a moment and then said, "Look, don't try and kill more than anyone else. Just do what you need to do to accomplish your mission. Understand?"

I lifted an eyebrow. That sounded remarkably humane for a veteran soldier. Stickman smiled disarmingly. "Your body count will rise over time. Trust me. Won't be long before you're the top killer on this moon."

I had to force myself not to flinch but instead gave my best, cocky smile. The mere thought of killing more humans turned my empty stomach. Stickman's eyes narrowed as his smile faded.

"Something wrong?"

My face had betrayed my mood. "I guess I'm just tired. But I've seen things down there. Things no man should ever see."

There was a connection between us at that moment. Veterans with a shared history of death and destruction. Brothers in arms. I wondered if it were even possible for a veteran with as many kills as Stickman had to have ever guessed that they were fighting other humans. Stickman sat back in his chair and grinned with a sigh. He knew I could feel it.

"Get back to your unit then. You're going down to

Betwi-Three next rotation. Give them hell, son."

I hesitated for a moment, then I snapped to attention and left. As I walked back to the berthing area, I realized that even if Stickman did know the truth, he would probably never admit it. I wished that he were going with us on this one. It would have been an honor to fight and, if needed, to die at his side.

***

The crew berthing on the *Elpida* was sparse, and each soldier had only a narrow bunk with a pull curtain for privacy. I lay on my bunk with my hands crossed behind my head. I recalled my conversations with the enemy soldier while my right leg rocked back and forth, causing the springs to creak annoyingly.

The privacy curtain was open, and other soldiers were sitting around repairing their armor and trying to polish it up for the next drop. I didn't give a shit about all that anymore. I ensured my equipment was serviceable, but I didn't try to get the gray regolith dust out of it or polish any scuffs.

I was wearing a tank top and my briefs. The air on the starship was dry and cool, but I wasn't cold. I stared at the Elysian flag pinned to the inner wall beside my bunk. It was the flag that Trille had given to me before I left. I unhooked it and slowly folded it up into a solid blue triangle. I slid it into a cubby and tried not to think of how everything it stood for was now a lie.

Selina slipped into my bunk and sat down on my legs. She was also in her sleep clothes. Lights out was in five minutes. I decided to go for it and tell her about what happened. I seriously doubted she would question me or turn me in. I pulled the curtain closed and sat up to whisper.

"You once told me you believed in the old stories about Acheron. Do you still believe them? That we're fighting humans and not bugs?"

She nodded, but her eyes narrowed suspiciously. I paused for a moment before continuing. "I believe them now. I've met the enemy and he was not a bug, he was a man no older than me."

From the confusion on her face, I knew Selina didn't

know whether to believe me or not. I slipped a hand inside my bed sheets and pulled out a three-circle placard I stole from the hidden control room on Betwi-Two. She recognized the symbol and touched the placard with her fingers. I waited for someone to pass by and then spoke just loud enough for her to hear.

"I was in single combat with one of their soldiers inside the western wall of their fortress. We became trapped in an underground airlock, not part of the fortress. He took off his helmet and even spoke the same language as us. Can you believe that shit?"

Her dark eyes widened not from excitement but from anger. "You're endangering our lives talking to me about this. I'm scheduled to return home with the Victory Squads."

"Someone must know what I've seen."

I held up a chip that I had concealed in my palm. She looked at it longingly as if it were a holy object.

"This is an interview I did with the enemy soldier. Try and get people to see it or whatever you think is the right thing to do."

Selina shook her head. "I never expected you, of all people, to come to me with something like this. I don't know what to say."

I stared into her eyes for a moment and then looked away. My foot was still rocking back and forth.

"War changes people, Selina. Especially when you meet the enemy and find out he's not some hideous alien, he's just like you. I'm probably going to be promoted again. After that, I'll lead the first wave of the B-Three invasion. The odds, if not the government, are against me."

"But you're one of the most experienced soldiers in the Army. Surely you won't be killed," she pleaded.

"Experience is only good for a few months; after that, your odds are about as good as a noob. You know that as well as I do. Most of my squad is heading back with you. I'm sure I was supposed to rotate back now, too."

Selina wrapped her arms around me and pulled me closer to her in a hug.

"I lied to you about my body count. I never killed any of

the enemy. I've always believed they were humans like us. I volunteered to come here just to prove this and now you have proved it for me."

I caressed her face with my hand. "How I envy you. I wish I had never killed anyone."

"What are you going to do on Betwi-Three? You'll have to fight, or you will die."

My blue eyes gave away my intentions, and she started to cry.

"You're never coming back, are you?"

I didn't answer; I just wiped away her tears. The flood was more than I could stop. We hugged tightly. I hadn't thought that what I was doing was suicidal until now. Volunteering to go off to some faraway moon and get killed while killing others seemed so romantic not that long ago. It was every kid's backyard dream; everyone who ever picked up a stick and pretended it was a laser gun. There were all those heroic holographic dramas with their dramatic music and an endless supply of ammo for the heroes to condition us into wanting to fight.

The real war was not like that at all. It was exhausting, stinky, and terrifying all the damn time. It was kill or be killed. It was losing the person next to you and still pressing the attack, even if that person was your lover, your best friend, or both. War was now a special kind of hell for me. I was no longer just exterminating heartless pests. I was taking human lives, and that was unconscionable.

"I'll do my best to get back."

She continued sobbing on my shoulder, and I held her tightly in my arms. She was the best thing that had ever happened to me, and I wanted to share a life with her now more than ever.

I sensed too late that someone was loitering outside the blanket wall as we talked. Two hands reached into my bunk and pulled me out. It was Hector, and he was angrier than I had ever seen him. He started beating the crap out of me. His face was red with rage, and his mouth was set in a snarl as he delivered blow after blow. I had fallen to the floor and struggled to get to my feet. Selina charged into Hector, not knowing who this soldier was, only to protect her man from him.

Finally, I got to my feet and landed a single punch to Hector's face with the chip embedded in my fist. Then, I pushed Hector into a nearby holographic training room. The door slid shut behind me, and I locked Selina out. I didn't want her any more involved than she already was. Hector looked around the room before raising his fists, ready to go at it again. I put the data chip into the control station, and the entire room lit up with the video from my interview. It was like we were all standing in the same room with Gaven.

Gaven's face was clearly human as he wore the bug army suit.

"Look at him, Hector! He's not a goddamn bug! He's human, just like you and me."

Hector looked around, confused for a moment. Then he lashed out at me.

"It's not real, Jered! The enemy is tricking you into not fighting them. All this," he waved at the glowing images on the walls, his voice cracking, "is a big lie. It's a trick to get you to show sympathy for the enemy."

I shook my head slowly. That thought had occurred to me before. What if I had been knocked out and the enemy had played an elaborate trick on me with human actors? There was no way I could rule it out. It was only a gut feeling on my part that convinced me I was right.

I used a handheld controller to skip forward to the part about the flag. Then, I skipped back to the warehouse, where the vehicles of the different sides were moving around crates of uniforms and weapons.

"It's not a ruse, Hector. The war is a lie. We aren't fighting bugs. We're fighting ourselves. All for what? Profit, that's what. Can't you see that?"

Hector stopped looking at the projections around him and focused on me. There was an unmistakable look of pity on his innocent face. I knew then that I couldn't convince my friend that he was wrong. That what we had believed growing up was all a terrible lie from our government. It was not an easy pill to swallow for anyone. Especially a First In First Out troop like Hector, who had never been in close combat with the enemy. I had never blasted open a bug's armor and saw what I now knew was a human's skeleton under the roasted flesh and yellow blood. How could anyone not exposed to the horrors of war truly understand what it was like?

"You used to be a patriot. I don't know what they did to you, but you're not the man I used to know anymore," Hector said, his voice low and measured.

Hector walked past me with a look of disgust on his face. I let him go. I couldn't do anything more to convince my old friend that he was wrong. Outside the holo room, Selina came to my side. I gave the data chip to her, and she discreetly slipped it into her waistband.

"He's probably going to turn you in," she said.

"Let him. What will they do to me, send me into battle?"

***

Later that night, Lacithe's security troops woke me up and inspected every inch of my gear. They wouldn't tell me what they were looking for, but I knew they wanted the chip I gave Selina. They didn't inspect her stuff, thankfully. Probably because Hector didn't know who she was. When the goons didn't find anything, they left as quickly as they had arrived. It took me a while to get back to sleep after that.

***

The next morning, I got my shaving kit out and covered my sullen face with white shaving cream. I looked at myself in the mirror and realized I looked as bad as I felt. My hair was cut short to uniform specifications, but the lines under my eyes seemed permanent. I looked twenty years older than I was.

As I dragged the razor across my cheek, I felt someone's presence and looked away from the mirror. It was Hector. The kid had a smug look on his face, as if he knew something I didn't. It was annoying, and after our last meeting, I was in no mood to deal with him now.

"What do you want?"

"I just wanted to see you again before I left."

I wiped off my razor on the gray towel around my neck and returned to shaving. "Going home so soon?"

"I want to stay and head down to B-Three with you. I hear it will be a hell of a big fight."

"Shame you can't join us."

He seemed oblivious to the sarcasm. I cleaned off my razor again and shook my head. "Say hello to Trille for me."

Hector smiled in that annoying way that I had always hated. As if he thought he was winning.

"Oh, I will. We're engaged."

I stopped shaving and stared at Hector in the mirror. The smile was insufferable now. I turned to face my former friend.

"I hope you have a long and happy life together. Maybe your kids will come here and fight like their old man."

Hector nodded in appreciation, completely ignorant of my dark sarcasm. "They will come here, I can promise you that. I hear you're promoting again."

"I'll be leading my squad during the invasion."

The jealous look on Hector's face sickened me.

"Man, how I envy you."

Hector suddenly remembered something and dug into his pocket until he pulled out a golden ring. He handed it to me. I recognized it immediately. It was my grandfather's combat ring that I had given Trille back in the world. A lifetime ago.

"Trille said to give this back to you. She thought it would bring you luck."

I took the ring before turning back around to continue shaving. "Goodbye, Hector."

Hector stepped back to leave, sighed, and said, "Goodbye." He turned on his heels and briskly walked down the corridor. As I watched him leave, I knew something wasn't right. Hector usually tried to make up with me after we had fought. He always wanted to be sure things were still good between us, but that goodbye had been said in relief. It was as if he didn't ever expect to see me again and was fine with it. I shrugged and finished my shave. If things went as I hoped, Hector and Trille's children would never come here to fight.

I looked at the ring on the metal shelf by my mirror as I

finished shaving. A part of me was grateful to have it back. Another darker part of me was sad that I might never see Trille again. I wondered if it would give me some good fortune. Where I was going, I'd need all the luck I could get.

Ioudas

22

The *Ioudas* hung in orbit of Betwi-Three like a dull needle poised to puncture the blue and white moon. The pipes and electrical conduits along the starship's sides were rusted from continued exposure to the sulfur volcanoes of the first moon. Betwi-Three was the ice ball moon the furthest away from Betweos. Long veins of frozen methane and other gasses crossed its surface irregularly. A tenuous atmosphere allowed fierce winds to create massive, globe-spanning snowstorms across the surface.

The deterioration of our ship was a metaphor for the failing Acheron Army. Its equipment and its soldiers were wearing thin from the war. It was never this apparent to me before. I was too involved in my misery to notice. There were days left in the campaign before Betweos moved out of reach. Before, the planet and its moons were closer to the enemy for an unbearably long stretch of time. This would be the last stand of the Acheron Army. Every starship, every piece of equipment, every soldier, and every weapon would be used to defend the frozen moon, wreaked by tidal forces from Betweos.

But none of that mattered to me now. All I could think about when I got back inside the outpost was the fact that Slik had been reported dead. I inquired up the chain and was finally told the truth by Hacker, who showed me pictures of Slik's body in the morgue at Graul. I think he was hoping for some kind of emotional outburst from me, given my insistence on seeing proof my friend was dead. But I didn't give that bastard the satisfaction. I just stared in silence at him, and then I left without a word.

At this point, I had only one person left from my old surface gang to fight for: Shen. As we transferred back to the Ioudas, I mostly kept to myself and tried to process Slik's death and meeting Jered. I would spend free time in the non-rotating center spine of the starship, watching the crew section rotate and staring out at the beautiful, swirling gas giant whose icy grip we all seemed to be captured by.

***

Inside the engine room of the Ioudas was a dark and foreboding place. There was no gravity, so you had to float along handholds to get where you wanted. A layer of black grime covered everything. There were few crewmen in the area, and I easily slipped past them to enter an even more secluded maintenance storage room. I wore my black inner armor suit, which afforded me perfect cover in the shadows as I waited for Shen to join me.

We had to constantly seek out new and secluded spots to screw or risk being caught. It had been a while since we had done it in Engineering. Shen hated the low gravity and the greasy walls. I considered all that bonus stimulation for what we would be doing.

A low rumble from nearby machinery and the occasional pressure release from above ensured this hiding spot was well-masked from prying eyes and ears. I turned my head upon hearing the dogs of the hatch opening. It was Shen, wearing her black service uniform with red piping as she floated into the room. We embraced and immediately started kissing and tearing each other's clothes off. Our naked bodies were immediately soaked with perspiration and floated as we fought for leverage in love's sweet dance.

***

I pulled myself free and stretched out, floating near the ceiling, spent and still breathing heavily. Shen flailed around, looking for her uniform pants. She found them and started dressing immediately while I floated there, relaxing in the dark. My eyes scanned the ceiling for the sign of a security camera I knew was up there somewhere. It was either off or broken because I couldn't see its steady red light.

"Do you think if we ever manage to return home, they will make us be RUTs?" Shen asked out of the blue.

I laughed. "Probably. But I doubt any of us will return."

"Really?" she asked.

"It's a one-way journey. There was never a return trip."

She seemed troubled by my answer, but I swear we'd discussed this a thousand times before. Nobody really expected to come home alive, but now that Slik was gone, I was all but convinced of it.

Shen spun around, trying to get a leg into her pants. I debated telling her what I had found under Graul when I was away. Would she turn me in? Would Hacker find some way to hurt me through her if he found out that I knew the entire war was a sham? I decided to get it off my chest and just tell her.

"I found something in the Western Wall area while trapped there."

She pulled up her pants and looked at me. I stared at her in the dark, and she squinted to see me. My voice was low, barely audible over the machinery's din.

"There's a Betweener Base under the fort. Perfectly preserved, complete with shipping documents and everything. Looks like it hasn't been used in hundreds of years."

I couldn't see any concern on her face, but I could hear it in her timid voice. "You didn't tell anyone, did you?"

"No, I'm not that stupid," I quipped.

She pulled on her top. I watched her as I spoke. "If the enemy ever captures that fort, they could find that hidden base. That would be something, wouldn't it?"

She seemed disinterested in what I was saying, more focused on sliding her boots on. I was still floating naked, gently caressing the chilled skin on my chest.

"I better not say anything more; they are probably listening," Shen said. She looked around the empty room and folded her arms over her chest.

"We're cool. I rewired the camera signal to the head."

She looked down at me and cracked a grin.

***

A few days later I hadn't seen Shen anywhere and was about to go looking for her. She had missed all our regular formations and was no longer in her bunk during sleep rotations. Whenever someone woke up and disappeared from the squad, it usually meant they had run afoul of Hacker. I was beginning to fear that's what had happened to her.

Sitting on my bunk, I was cleaning my armor for the next battle when I heard someone approach. I glanced up as Polit Officer Hacker approached me with his polished boots. Speak of the devil. I stood up at attention. Hacker was wearing his stiff black dress uniform with the red piping. The cut was crisp and fitted perfectly to his lean form.

Hacker took the leg armor from me and brought it up to examine. His dark, impenetrable eyes drew slowly over the weathered armor, and his gloved hand ran along the smooth outer surface. His head cocked at an angle that suggested approval, and he handed the piece back to me.

"At ease, Sergeant."

I relaxed my stance but not my guard. I looked Hacker in the eye.

"I understand you had quite an adventure down on B-2. Something about being trapped by a landslide?"

"Yes, sir. It's all in my after-action report. I didn't think you were interested."

Hacker lowered his voice and stared deep into my soul. "I know you've seen the Betweener station below our Graul Outpost."

I didn't so much as blink. I wouldn't give any if he were looking for some sign of weakness.

"What I don't know is who else has seen the base? Care to elaborate on your story, Sergeant? Did your dead friend Slik see it?"

I didn't respond.

Hacker narrowed his eyes and got right up into my personal space, the same thing he did to new recruits. I never let it bother me then, and I don't let it bother me now.

"I know what you saw. Do you know how I know?"

I didn't budge. I just kept staring ahead at infinity. Fuck

this asshole.

"Sergeant Shen informed me all about it."

That nearly got a rise out of me. I continued to stare straight ahead, even as I died inside. I didn't think she'd rat me out like that. He must have promised her a return ticket.

Hacker backed away from me slowly, turned smartly on his heels, and left. I let out my breath and noticed my hands were balled tightly into fists. I had been seconds away from swinging at the Polit Officer but stood my ground. I didn't give the man the satisfaction of knowing how much of a gut punch I had been dealt. After Hacker had left the deck, I sat down and tossed my leg armor across the room as hard as possible. It clattered loudly on the metal deck, causing the nearest soldiers to open their curtains to see what was happening.

I had been trying to find a way to get Hacker since I was abducted into the army. I hated everything about the man. I hated his sickly, pallid skin. I hated his naturally red hair for its in-your-face reminder of the Acheron Army's primary color. I hated his smug, above-everyone attitude. But most of all, I hated the man for being The Man incarnate.

How anyone could be that much up the state's ass and still be breathing was completely beyond me. Maybe he was a robot? The perfect tool of the government, willing to execute anyone to maintain order. Fuck that! I'll show him who's really in charge of this God-forsaken war. It wasn't the government, and it wasn't that hack.

Sitting in my bunk with the curtains shut, I used my combat knife to carve a message into my chest plate. Something nobody would understand except for Hacker. Three goddamned circles. Underneath the circles, I painted in blood red - "Destroyer."

***

An hour before the scheduled prep time for my drop, I snuck back into the engine storage room where Shen and I had been. I was wearing my all-black, rubberized suit liner and towing a satchel in the microgravity. After I entered the room, I activated a localized EMP stick and pointed it at the security camera on the ceiling. The red light went off instantly. Then I took out the bundle of rifle energy packs I had stolen from the armory. I had been taking them for months and keeping them hidden from prying eyes. Nobody had reported them missing because we were at war, and energy packs were distributed like candy bars.

The bundle was rigged so that when I activated a fuse, it would set all the packs off in a deadly explosive chain. Running through this room was the main coolant line for the star drive. Rip a big enough hole into this baby, and the entire drive will overheat and ignite the ship like a flare in the darkest night.

There wouldn't be time to get clear of the ship. Everyone left on board would be killed. And that, I knew, included Polit Officer Hacker. The *Ioudas* would fly in formation for this drop with a second transfer ship. The *Acheras* would be dropping her soldiers simultaneously in a last-ditch effort to overwhelm the enemy defenses and take the moon.

The two starships would be a spitting distance apart for the drop. If I blew up the *Ioudas*, the *Acheras* would not be able to escape damage and would be racked by enough shrapnel to be destroyed. There would be no way for anyone to return home. Those who were not killed in the fight would die on this third moon, eventually.

Shen would be on the *Acheras*. She would be killed, too. A part of me deeply regretted that. But Hacker had turned her, and she was unable to resist him. At one time, back on Acheron, I had fought for her survival. Fought to protect all of my clan from the RUTS. Even after I became a trooper, I fought to protect my clan from death at the hands of the enemy. Combat had taken most of them now. I slowly realized that it was my duty to kill them all. I aimed to end the war by ending everyone I had ever known. I was Gaven the Destroyer.

If my plan worked, I would end this fight with Hacker. I set the remote and patted the bomb for luck. Then I left the room, never to return.

Elpida

23

My unit reported for duty in our medium-weight battle armor. That could mean only one thing. We wouldn't be jumping on Betwi-Three. We would be manning armored vehicles. Tanks were only used on the third moon for some damn reason that I had long forgotten. I hated being trapped inside them during a battle. I had been to B-3 once before as a runner, responsible for personally taking coded drives and maps to the area commander.

I had ridden inside the cramped, white walls of the tank with the crew of three who had worked the main guns, steered the lumbering beast, and commanded it from atop the copula. There wasn't enough room for a proper passenger, but they had let me curl up inside the main turret if I promised to stay out of everyone's way.

Rattling around inside that metal coffin had made me yearn for suit warfare, where I could roam free across the ice fields and see the battle unfold before me. Trapped inside a tank with no windows and no idea what was going on around me was a new kind of hell that I had never imagined before. So much of the war was like that for me now. If I had known about how nasty the whole affair was, I might never have signed up for it, and I'm pretty sure I wouldn't have glamorized the fighting. All those Capture the Flag games with Hector and our other friends would never have happened. I would have found some other outlet for my energy, like organized sports.

But that wasn't how my life played out. I had trained with corn stalks and sticks until I was old enough to join the army. By the time I was actually in combat, it was too late. The insanity and violence of war were more than I could have ever dreamed of as a kid. It was not glamorous or heroic in any way. It was tiring and terrifying, and I never realized how pointless it was.

Now that I understood it was a manufactured war created by the very companies that designed and built the weapons both sides used, I could no longer participate in wanton death and destruction.

Sitting in a metal chair and listening to the tank battalion commander drone on about objectives, I remembered the day I met Saburo at the recruiting station. We were both so young and innocent, especially big old Saburo. I had felt an immediate kinship with him. Something was comforting in knowing that the gentle giant would have my back when the fighting got intense—good old Saburo.

The smiling image of my friend on that day was replaced with the torn and bloody carcass littered all over the storage room on Betwi-One. My eyes had long ago lost their sparkle, and now I stared blankly ahead, devoid of emotion. I wanted to cry for Saburo, but tears would not come.

I was jarred out of my thoughts by the shipboard PA.

"Attention the ship, attention the ship. Sergeant Jered reported to Morale Officer Lacithe's office. That is all."

I heard my name and snapped up out of my chair.

***

Standing before Lacithe's office door, I touched the release pad with my hand, and it slid aside. The Morale Officer was sitting calmly at his desk, dressed in black. His pale white face looked up with a hint of annoyance. The blue hair was thick and spiked on the top of his head. I always hated his blue hair. It was so over the top.

"Come in, Sergeant."

I entered the cramped room and stood at attention as the door slid shut behind me.

"Sergeant Jered reporting as ordered, sir."

Lacithe sat there looking at me for a long moment. I kept my eyes fixed forward. I could hear the slight nasal sound of the man breathing.

"You're being promoted to Command Sergeant Major. Congratulations."

I was startled enough to glance down at him. Lacithe shrugged as if he had nothing to do with it.

"At ease, Command Sergeant Major."

I relaxed and looked into the man's crystal-clear blue eyes. There was no life in those eyes—just the heartless, indifferent eyes of someone who didn't care about anyone else.

"Your unit will be going in with the Eighty-sixth Armor Regiment. This is the final battle of this orbit. There is only one objective. Take back the moon at all costs. Understood?"

My voice echoed off the metal walls. "Yes, sir."

Lacithe stood up and approached his desk to stand before me. He was close enough to be in my personal space, so the attempt at intimidation didn't affect me. He moved in closer. We were eye to eye, and neither one of us blinked.

"I know what you saw on Betwi-Two."

I didn't flinch. I knew there was nothing Lacithe could do to me worse than send me back into combat.

"That Betweener base was abandoned years ago. Every cycle builds over the top of the previous one's battlefield. No land is sacred in this system unless you win it on the return."

I listened but didn't react to what I was being told. The Morale Officer didn't know what I had seen down there. He was just guessing.

"The enemy usually thrives in tunnels. I'm surprised they haven't used the old bases for laying their eggs."

He didn't know. How could he not know the truth? That must mean the truth is unknown to everyone fighting.

"You didn't see any evidence of that down there, did you? Because that would be valuable intelligence."

I shook my head slowly. Lacithe backed away and seemed bored again. He circled behind his desk and opened a drawer. Pulling out a command sergeant major stripes, he set them on the desk.

"You were supposed to return home with the others in your squad. But I can't afford to lose you. Not now. You're our best fighter, and we need your help to take back this moon."

I remained stone-faced.

"Go ahead, take the stripes and report for duty," Lacithe said.

I scooped up the stripes and came to attention.

"I don't expect to see you again unless we are victorious. Is that understood?"

My stoic expression nearly broke. That was direct.

I did an about-face and touched the sensor on the door. The door slid open, and I drew a breath of fresh air from the corridor outside.

"Happy hunting, Sergeant Major," Lacithe said, mockingly.

I stepped out of the room and headed down the hallway, fists balling tightly.

                                    ***

The LIFO troops were boarding the shuttle that would take them back home on another transfer ship. A long line of still raw recruits was being sent back on the eve of perhaps the most important battle. When they returned to Elysia, they claimed to have been there when we won back the moon. I held a triangular folded Elysian flag as I scanned faces for Hector. Every dark-haired kid turned to look when I shouted his name. Only one of them was Hector, and he turned around as I approached him.

"Take this, it's Trille's. She loaned it to me before I left," I said coldly.

Hector took the flag from me, his face confused.

"I may not return; I wanted her to have it."

The line moved again, and Hector's group began to board. He held up the flag and nodded back to me. Then he turned around and disappeared inside. I knew I'd probably never see my childhood friend again, and I was oddly okay with that. The long line of soldiers seemed never-ending.

I had to find Selina next before she boarded. I scanned

the faces among the soldiers as they strode past me. Every cycle had survivors. People sent back to ensure the homeland wouldn't lose hope in a seemingly endless war.

Selina was one of the lucky ones, and I desperately needed her to make it out so that she could break the news about the cover-up and show the world that they were fighting humans and not bugs. I was slowly coming to grips with the fact that I would never return home. I would never see the clear blue skies over green and yellow corn fields, never breathe clean air, never see my parents again, and never know a life without war.

I saw a gray-haired woman up ahead and made my way to her by pressing past other soldiers. She turned around and saw me and a hand came up to her face. She nearly started bawling right there. We embraced in a hug that I never wanted to end.

"I thought I'd never see you again," she whispered.

I held her tightly. "Lacithe doesn't know the truth. You've got to get into the company – SVK Industries. They run both sides of the war. Even the military is unaware."

She nodded as we parted. Her eyes started welling with tears.

"Jered, I have to tell you something."

I held her at arm's length. "I'm pregnant," she said.

She tried to smile but was stopped by my astonished look. I grabbed her head and pulled her to me in a deep kiss, followed by another close hug.

"I love you," I whispered.

"I love you too."

The line started moving again, and everyone filed past them into the departing shuttle. Selina backed away. She had to board. I wouldn't let go of her hands. I kept staring hard at her, trying to fix her face into my memory. The line got smaller behind them.

"I have to go," she said. She let go of me and backed away. I reluctantly released her. I wanted to run after her and join her on the shuttle, but I couldn't. There were cameras throughout the hallway, and at the other end of them was no doubt Morale Officer Lacithe. Watching.

Selina boarded the shuttle and looked back at me one last time. She was too far away to see my wet eyes. I was barely holding myself together. The airlock seal slid shut, and I could no longer see my love. I glanced up again at the monitors and turned away. She's pregnant! A small part of me would live on, and with any luck, that kid would never have to come to this terrible place in space, at least not to fight.

***

I sat on my bunk with a metal chest plate in my lap. I carved three circles into the gray paint with my combat knife. The symbol of the Peacer movement was the symbol of the company responsible for the war. Nobody around me made that connection. If they did, they wisely chose to ignore it.

Drop time was in two hours. It seemed like an eternity. I had way too much time to think about it, to ponder about If I could fight anymore. To think about how I would avoid it for as long as possible. To consider the fact that not fighting might lead to my immediate death by fratricide. I remembered the night before my first drop. I had tossed and turned in my bunk, never able to sleep. I kept thinking it might be my last few hours alive. Do you remember your entire life, the good times and the bad? Do you regret things you did or didn't do? Do you ponder the afterlife? Do you pray to a higher being that you might live? I did none of those things. I had just laid there staring at the ceiling and waiting for the night shift to end. I had listened to the mechanical sounds of the ship's engines and the air vents blowing. Eventually, I became convinced that I wouldn't die. I was still a young, confident man who believed I was invincible. No matter what happened on the next combat drop, it would not be me who was killed.

My heavy eyes took in the other soldiers, preparing their armor for the drop. They were all veterans of many drops and countless battles. Each of them had their routines, and none looked around and noticed that I was watching them. Some listened to fast, loud music. Others seemed to repeatedly tell themselves a mantra in their heads while a few of them knelt in prayer.

I have never been particularly religious. I went through the motions on the day of rest and recited passages from the book, but I never thought about what happened after I died. I was too busy living this life to ponder what came after it.

Tonight, it seemed, was my night to ponder it. I wasn't concerned about where I would go or if I would have to answer for my actions in this life. I knew that what I had set in motion was blasphemous to my people's beliefs and treasonous for a soldier, but I also knew that dead men couldn't be tried for treason. Tonight, I decided that if I were to be judged for my actions in the afterlife, I would be content to accept whatever fate I was given. For I was doing the morally right thing.

Betwi-Three, Acheron Front

24

Betwi-Three was the farthest moon from the silver gas giant of Betweos. A frozen ball of blue and white ice with a thin atmosphere and no heat source. Its surface was ancient and fractured with fissures in the ice that sometimes dipped kilometers below the surface. Fall into one of those, and you'll never get out alive.

Sidsini Base was a series of frozen trenches that snaked from a former river bed. The tendrils of frozen water ran parallel to an icy ridge line along the base of a mountain. A wide, flat sea of blue ice extended away to the moon's shortened horizon. I'd never seen an ocean before, but they told me it was similar in vastness.

Ammunition and power packs littered the trench. A fine layer of frost covered them and the suited troopers standing sentry. My squad was spread out every ten paces, weapons perched over the top of the trench. Our suits were hastily painted white on their upper surfaces. The dark gray paint was still visible, making them look weathered despite not having been on station for long. A few of them were covered in thermal blankets designed to mask their power signatures. It was an accidental side benefit that they also provided an insulating layer over the cold metal of the suits.

Steam clouds trailed upward from behind our helmets but froze before getting far. The frozen water vapor fell onto the armor suits, covering them like tiny snowflakes. There was a growing storm on the horizon; it had already blocked out the inky black sky. Betweos itself lingered above us, filling two-thirds of the sky. I never got tired of staring at the silver and gray clouds of the gas giant. It was like a hulking, silent sentry that watched over every battle with baleful indifference.

My chest plate was etched with the three-circle design Jered and I had found on the second moon. The white paint didn't obscure it. I wanted to just use paint for it but hadn't managed to steal it before heading to the surface. You couldn't see the circles unless you were standing close to me, which was probably a good thing, given how Hacker scrutinized everything we did. I hid it from his eyes with a blanket.

The storm was quickly moving in on us. I studied the horizon using my internal viewer screens, switching from radar to IR and back to visual in a consistent pattern, looking for any signs of an enemy drop.

The situation finally earned mentioning to my command.

"This is Redstar Five. The storm is closing fast on our position. No sign of the enemy. Over."

A burst of static emphasized the poor atmospherics. "Copy Redstar Five. Standby for seekers. Enemy contacts at the outer perimeter."

I acknowledged him and switched back to my squad freq.

"Heads up, seeker sponges. Form on me."

The five nearest troopers ambled over to me in their four-armed battle suits. Each had a red number stenciled over the sloppy paint job on their upper torso. I eyed them with my standard video. They looked like motley veterans to me. Too bad my enthusiasm for killing had waned lately. I would have been proud of them.

"Enemy contacts at the outer perimeter. Expect seekers any time now. Check your flares."

Every trooper had a cluster of pipes that contained anti-seeker flares. We all hit switches on our upper arms that activated the flares. I looked each trooper over with the scrutiny of a veteran. Many of them had reactive armor plates attached to their regular armor, making them look like testosterone-filled badasses.

One of them had a large, articulated canon on his back. The man tested its auto-tracking on his comrades. It was more than a little unnerving to have a huge barrel swing in your direction, even if it didn't fire on you. The man seemed satisfied it was operational and secured it above his head like some ancient banner carrier.

"Alright, take your position. It's playtime," I said.

We climbed on the icy rim of the trench and carefully aimed our weapons towards the approaching storm. The man with the cannon had an assistant loader responsible for reloading the cannon with energy packs. He had them attached to his suit and arms like extra armor plating.

My inner suit was supplemented by a fur-lined helmet designed to help keep me warmer in the hostile cold of the moon. My breath still froze coming out of my mouth as I stared dull-eyed at the screens. Every suit had its feel and smell. Each one is uniquely balanced with our load out. This one fit me the best of all the suits I had worn since arriving at the front. It was the only one that felt like an extension of my body. Like a well-worn jacket or a breather mask that fits the contours of your face like a glove.

My tracker lit up with multiple bogies. "Seekers, incoming!" I yelled into my mic.

Troopers started opening fire out of reflex. They could no more nail a seeker than hit a flying insect, but that didn't stop them from trying. Flares started shooting off around us as the tiny rocket-propelled munitions tried to break our lines and blow us into oblivion.

Seekers were finned, explosive-tipped rockets designed to locate a trooper and take him out autonomously. They were a deadly standoff weapon that induced fear and broke down discipline along our lines. Our troopers all hated them. I sprayed the thin air before me with rounds and took out one of the frightening weapons.

Brilliant white flares lured most seekers up and away from the trenches, where they blew themselves up, hitting the incandescent magnesium. One poor trooper was not as lucky as the others. His flares malfunctioned, and a seeker locked onto his center mass and impaled him. The insidious seeker warhead split in two, one half tunneled up through his spine to explode near his head from the inside and the other reamed itself down one leg and exploded. Bits of bone and blood sprayed everywhere and froze on the ice around him. It made a disgusting mess and chilled everyone who saw the carnage. The poor sap let out a sickening scream before dying. It echoed in everyone's helmet as they fought on.

The last seeker exploded above them into a flare, and the battle got quiet inside my helmet. The winds from the storm buffeted against me as I tried to make out enemy contacts to shoot. I knew they were coming - it was as sure as death.

I tapped the top of my head with my right arm. It was my visual signal to the others around me that the enemy was close at hand. The winds picked up even more, and anything not secured began to flap around or blow away. I felt something tapping my right leg and realized one of my armor shields was loose. I bent down far enough to slap it securely against my leg. Before I could right myself Elysian soldiers started materializing through the snowy winds.

Flashes of light began flaring up randomly as the enemy started firing. My squad immediately returned fire in kind. The air around us quickly filled with the crisscrossing beams of deadly energy weapons. I got off several kill shots before finally ducking beneath the rim and letting my blast shield absorb some hits.

I rose and leveled another enemy soldier as he was about to jump into my trench. The dead man fell in front of me, face up. I could see the outline of his face inside his helmet. It was not clear enough to recognize him, but all I could see was the face of my new friend, Jered.

Unnerved by the image, I pushed the dead man's body

away and refocused on the fight. Fewer enemy soldiers were advancing, and my squad mates easily took down all of them. My screens started shorting out and then went blank for a couple of seconds. That could have meant one thing: Battle tanks.

My screens winked back on and painted large targets approaching through the storm. Tanks always hit us with EM bursts before their attack to fry all the electronics of an unprotected suit, hoping to catch someone off guard by not having their radiation shields up. When the tanks first appeared on the battlefields of Betwi-Two, they caused unprecedented death and destruction by simply suffocating countless numbers of our troopers in their suits.

Eventually, our techs figured out how to counter them, and now all they got was a temporary blackout before the tanks engaged. It was a tip-off that I was not prepared for. There had been no mention of battle tanks in the pre-attack briefings.

The ground began to rumble with the weight of the tracked metal monsters as they lumbered closer. I waved to my squad and made a circular motion with my hand, the signal to expect a vertical attack. Elysian forces nearly always sent in tanks and deployed soldiers with retro packs from above. I'm told air and ground combined attack was as old as armed combat.

The high winds continued to blow through the battlefield. I tried to brace myself behind a shield. It protected me from a near miss from one of the battle tanks. The wind speeds hampered an aerial attack. Maybe we'll get lucky, and they won't risk coming out.

I slid into the trench and kept my weapon pointing up, just in case. Before I could take two steps the skies parted with multiple Elysian soldiers screaming down on us with retros flaring. I squeezed off several shots, nailing at least one poor soul right between his legs. Another enemy soldier got off a decent hit on my shoulder armor plates. The armor was heaviest on top for such attacks and didn't penetrate. I returned fire immediately, and the hapless blue and white figure was blown apart and fell in a sick rain of blood and bits of armor.

Fighting in the trench was intense as the battle tanks lumbered closer. I knew once they got over my trench, they would be at the main fort in a matter of minutes. I had to take out as many as possible now, or we would suffer tremendous losses later.

I fought off another hovering enemy soldier and then proceeded to prepare an anti-tank round as the blunt nose of the first tank appeared over the top of me. I had one, maybe two attempts to disable the tank before it moved past. The armor on their bellies was just about impenetrable by Acheron weapons. My only chance was to hit the rocker arms where the treads attached to the main body and disable it.

My first shot glanced off the bottom of the tank and impacted the ice trench causing one of the inner walls to collapse in a crumble of ice stones. The tank teetered on the edge and started to fall into the trench. I took a second shot at the inside attachment point of the tilted tread. It was blown away completely, disabling the tank above me.

The trooper with the cannon seized the opportunity and started blasting away at the struck tank. I scrambled out of the way and watched briefly as the tank exploded into a molten pile of metal. Sometimes, war was beautiful. I praised my gunner and approached the trench to attack a second tank.

***

I slogged down an icy trench until I encountered another gunner team. Shen and her loader, Jade, hustled into a new firing position. I followed them and stood guard over them as Shen lined up her cannon to get the next tank as it crawled to the edge of our trench. Jade loaded the breech with an armor-piercing round and patted Shen's helmet.

Shen squeezed off the round, and it spiraled into the tank, gutting it like a hunted animal. The Elysian crew fell out of it, covered in glowing plasma. I picked them off with my rifle, and then the three of us were on the move again, trying to get in range to fire on the next tank.

Shen pulled herself over the nearest trench wall and aligned her cannon on an approaching tank. Jade struggled to get a round free and loaded as the tank looked closer.

"Hurry, I'm gonna miss it!" Shen spat into her microphone.

Jade responded with a helmet tap, and Shen fired.

The round clipped the front tread section and blew a massive gash in the side of the tank. Crewmen jumped out, firing hand weapons at us. I quickly dispatched them, their lifeless bodies falling into the icy pit. The tank was stalled over the trench and acted like a bridge for advancing troops to cross.

"Aim for the wall ahead of the tank and take it out," I directed.

Shen waited for Jade to reload her cannon.

"Firing."

The second shot destroyed the face of the wall, and the battle tank slipped into the trench. I picked off several Elysian soldiers trying to run across the top of the burning tank.

"Put another round into the rear." I hollered into my mic.

Jade tapped Shen's head and sat back. Shen fired the third shot, and the three of us immediately started to move as the tank burned bright as a star.

Snow pounded our armor from the high winds and clung to it like white mud as we hurried to the next battle tank. I covered our advance with my rifle from above. The location where we had fired the three shots was destroyed by a shell that sent burning metal and chips of ice everywhere in an explosion.

Shen and Jade fell into position to take a shot on a new battle tank coming around the burning one. She had to sit up to get the angle she needed. Her four arms balanced her as she aimed the massive cannon barrel. I grabbed Jade and tossed him aside. Then I kicked Shen's legs out from under her as a seeker whipped past us and impacted behind her. She cursed and tried to sit upright to get her shot. She looked down, and I could see several jagged pieces of shrapnel in her leg armor. She ignored the damage and continued lining up her shot.

It didn't line up the way she wanted it to. She continued

cursing. Jade had loaded the cannon and offered his body as a balancing point for the weapon. Shen rested the barrel across Jade's armored back and took the shot. They were a fantastic team to watch in action.

The shot struck the tank, but not fatally, and its massive cannon barrels tracked towards us to return our fire.

"Dammit, I could have had him!"

I aimed at the tank's fire control cluster and blasted it with a continuous stream of fire. The tank's armor was weak around the sensor and eventually failed. Shen and Jade scrambled out of the way as the tank fired blindly at us. We were tossed like dolls into the hard ice trench below.

We managed to get up as more Acheron troopers passed us, heading for the tank. I pushed on a metal hatch against the inner wall of the trench, and it opened.

"Come on, we stopped their advance. That's good enough for now."

Shen and Jade followed me inside a narrow corridor that led back into the main structure of Sidsini Base. A transfer shuttle was waiting to take the wounded back to orbit. I pointed to Shen's leg and then directed her to take the shuttle out. She resisted, but Jade pushed her along, reminding her that her suit was compromised and she couldn't fight until it was repaired.

I could tell she was feeling pain in her leg as the adrenaline of combat began to wear off. She turned to look back at me before I returned to the fight. A thought crossed my mind that I might not ever see her again. It was a common thought for a trooper, and I tried my best to forget it.

Betwi-Three, Elysian Front

25

The only surviving battle tank to reach the Acheron main line was in front of my squad. The tank opened fire on the Acheron base's walls and, within minutes, cracked a hole large enough for our soldiers to penetrate.

"Command, this is Alpha Squad. We have opened the wall at sector two-five-niner," I said over comms.

Static burst in my ears as a different, stoic male voice responded. "Copy Alpha. Press on with your attack."

Was that Lacithe's voice? It figured that bastard would be going with us for the victory battle. A disturbing thought crept into my consciousness. *What if he was here to ensure I didn't return?*

I shook my head to clear it.

Looking over my shoulder at the dozen soldiers under my command, nobody seemed interested in storming the breach. "We press on, people!"

Again, nobody stepped up to be first. I turned around with my back to the enemy—something you're never supposed to do in combat.

"Look, this is why we signed up, right? For the chance to serve our planet. It's time to serve."

I pointed to a young soldier nearest to me. "Start your advance, Sergeant. I'll call in more heavy support." The woman lowered her combat shield and waved to the soldiers behind her.

"Second Squad, you heard the man. Move out, people!"

Six soldiers got to their feet and started heading over the top of the trench towards the gaping hole in the Bug Army's wall. The gunner on the battle tank covered them as the storm winds continued to howl. Some soldiers were blown off their feet on the ice and snow but got back up and pressed on.

Within minutes they were firing on Acheron troops who had come to the wall's defense on the inside. Colored plasma beams crisscrossed the area in a surreal light show. I looked away from it, ducking behind the tank.

Another NCO slid in behind the tank next to me.

"Get Third Squad up here and give me a live count," I barked at him. The man waved his hand and headed off around the other side of the tank.

I switched comm channels to talk to the tank commander.

"Thunder Four, this is Alpha Squad. Head for the breach."

"Copy Alpha, ready to roll."

"Outstanding. Wait out."

I moved to the other side of the tank as the NCO returned. "Live count is one fiver, Sergeant."

"Mount up, you're going in behind us."

Third Squad began climbing up the sides of the battle tank and hanging on to the external rails, their weapons drawn. I returned to where another squad leader was hunkered down in the snow.

"Binc, I'll need to use what's left for backup. You're in charge. If we get pushed back or overrun, you engage. Copy that?"

Sergeant Binc looked at me as if I were insane.

"That's suicide!"

"This is war, Sergeant."

"If you're overrun, I'm getting my people the hell out of here."

I knew she could see my face through the shield. My eyes were wide open. "They'll have your ass for cowardice in the face of the enemy."

She shook her head and stared at the three circles on my chest plate.

"You're insane, Sergeant."

I smiled toothily, "Perhaps, but I'm also in charge."

Binc was aghast as I laughed.

"Thunder Four, move out!" I ordered as I turned around and grabbed onto a handrail on the back of the tank. The battle tank ambled forward, guns blazing.

***

I rode the battle tank closer to the wall breach. Enemy return fire brushed off several soldiers from the tank. From what I could see, the resistance was weakening. The tank bulldozed its way through the wall, making an even larger hole for my soldiers to flood inside.

"Outstanding, Thunder Four! Keep firing."

The tank responded, but the noise and cannon concussions drowned them out. Time seemed to stand still as the gunfire lit up the area in a chaotic death storm. I became lost in the wonder of the light show as explosions overlaid on each other in a beautiful display of power and death.

I was finally knocked out of my reverie when an enemy round impacted the far side of the battle tank. The shock wave knocked almost all the soldiers off, save for me. My arm was locked around a handhold as my body was pulled away and then back against the tank with a thud that nearly knocked me out.

"Thunder Four, Thunder Four. What's your status over?"

A new voice answered, yelling over the noise of battle. "Guidance is out fires under control. Commander and driver are dead."

"Keep moving. Get me closer."

"Sarge, we have no guidance."

"Just move it straight, soldier. That's an order."

"Copy."

The tank lurched forward, crushing the base of the first wall as it rolled over the debris. I waved for others to join me on the side of the tank as it rumbled past them. Nobody took me up on the free ride offer. Finally, a weary Sergeant Putao pulled himself up next to me.

"Everyone back on the tank, we're going in," I commanded the others.

Putao shook his head inside his suit. "Sarge, this tank's going to blow any second."

I pushed my head into Putao's faceplate.

"This tank won't blow until I get off, understand?"

Putao could see the rage on my face. He nodded inside his helmet as he turned to help another soldier climb onto the tank. Several more soldiers did the same, and before long, a dozen of us were hanging from the still-smoldering tank.

An Acheron anti-tank crew working from inside the base opened fire on us. The incendiary round barreled inside the massive beast and exploded. Six soldiers were killed instantly as their bodies were torn apart when the tank's main battery ignited. Everyone hanging outside the tank was blown off and fell onto the hard ice. I found myself on the ground as the tank came to a stop and fell inwards with a thunderous crash. Ice splintered and cracked around the dead beast.

With our cover blown, we pushed forward into the meat grinder of the Acheron Army. Dozens of Elysian soldiers were cut down like I used to destroy milky columns of weeds on the farm with a weak cutter. Frozen blood and shattered suits littered the battlefield. I watched the slaughter helplessly from my back. My suit had lost power when I had fallen off the tank. I fought to regain control before the enemy guns turned on me and other moving targets.

***

Hiding behind the cooking tank for cover, I finally got my comms working.

"Third Squad, move up and hold your fire," I ordered.

There was no immediate response from Binc. Blowing snow threatened to start burying us if we didn't get moving. I was about to shoot around her head to get her attention when she finally answered. She was probably pissed that I was still alive.

"Copy that, Sergeant."

I could see her signaling her soldiers with a wave, and they all slowly got up and prepared their weapons for an assault.

"Third Squad, form on me. Stay low and sharp. Fire on my signal," her deeper-than-normal command voice said.

Powder blue and white suits climbed up and over the icy walls of the trench as the squad slowly advanced toward the stricken tank like metallic zombies. Finally, the color of our suits matched the terrain we fought.

***

I watched the Third squad advance and bit my lower lip to force myself to focus on anything but the fact that I was probably about to die. The nameplate of a kid sitting beside me read Trevens. I pointed to his side of the tank.

"The enemy should be advancing on your side. Can you see them coming?"

Trevens edged his helmet around the massive tread of the tank.

"You're right, sarge. A swarm of them damn things are coming. How'd you know?"

I shook myself for a moment as I calmed down. Nerves, man, they never leave you alone.

"They're not bugs, kid. They are doing exactly what I would do. Because they're all humans, just like you and me."

Behind his face shield, I could see the kid's eyes as big as platters. It made me laugh because he reminded me of myself when I first got here. My laughter confused the kid. I'm sure he thought I was a madman after that. I waited a moment for my shakes to calm down.

"Just kidding, kid. This war's getting to me."

Trevens managed a weak grin, but I could see he was fixated now on the Peacer symbol on my chest.

"Get ready, we're going to glass those fuckers."

Trevens charged his rifle with a glorious smile on his youthful face. It sickened me to the point where my shakes started up again.

Betwi-Three, Elysian Front

26

Sergeant Binc's squad reached Thunder Four's still-burning shell and quickly engaged the Acheron troops in hand-to-hand fighting. Plasma guns were shot at point blank, but mostly, it was a steel-on-steel melee in the oldest known form of battle. I used the lasing bayonet more than anything as all my comrades fought for our lives against the four-armed enemy.

The Acheron suits held the advantage in a one-on-one fight, but the odds were even when more than two of us attacked one of the bug soldiers. The snowstorm started dumping huge, white flakes on the battlefield as we killed the enemy with brutal force.

The ground was soon slick with frozen red and yellow blood. I fought defensively, preferring to assist others than take the lead and often letting the other soldier have the killing shot. It was not how I was used to fighting, and I began taking more blows than I was delivering. My nervousness subsided once the fighting started, which was a relief, but I knew I couldn't avoid a fight much longer.

Before I could even begin to think about the ramifications of fighting back, I found myself jabbing the business end of my rifle into the bug-eyed helmet of a hapless Acheron soldier. When the helmet burst, so did the unfortunate man's head. The yellow mess that had been someone's head fractured into pieces as the body fell backward.

I pushed on over the dead Acheron man and immediately started exchanging blows with the next unfortunate soul. Time seemed to slow down for me as it often did in the heat of battle. I could anticipate the enemy's moves a second before anyone else, resulting in another dead Acheron man. My anticipation was not due to superior skills other than simple combat experience. The more time you have logged fighting, the better your skills become and the greater your chances of surviving.

As the latest victim fell forward, I glanced aside and saw hundreds of Acheron soldiers flooding out of the holes in the fort walls and into an equal number of Elysian soldiers who had advanced to support us. I had never been in a close-order battle with this many participants. It was terrifying and exhilarating at the same time. A glancing blow rocked my shoulder, which snapped my attention back to the killing task.

I fired a spray shot, and two Acheron soldiers exploded; their fractured armor and splattered guts covered everyone around them. Out of the cloud of debris and snow came a new foe standing on the remains of the previous corpses.

I looked up at the nearly silhouetted figure. He pulled up his rifle but didn't take a shot at me. Across the breastplate of the bug soldier was the familiar three circles of the Elysian Peacer movement. I knew instinctively that it was Gaven.

The figure held his fire and then reached out with one of his lower arms to pull me up on the pile of dead soldiers. I accepted the hand and stood toe-to-toe with him. I couldn't see inside the insect-like eye domes, but I knew it was my friend.

Death and destruction raged around us as we, two brothers in arms, embraced. Gaven used his superior strength to pull me around, and soon, we were back-to-back, each fighting the other's backside. I was the first to fire on the other Acheron soldiers; Gaven quickly followed, shooting Elysian soldiers. Before either of us could make sense of what was happening, we were both firing on our soldiers as much as the others.

Confusion spread around us as neither side knew how to handle a rogue soldier who was just as capable of killing his own as the enemy. Eventually, anger from both sides coalesced into action. Both sides began firing on Gaven and me as we managed to defend ourselves with alarming ease.

The war had made both of us expert killers and now the architects of the war would pay for that sin. The two of us opened up a steady stream of death that leveled every soldier on both sides for several meters around us. Bodies fell like trees from the center of an explosion. An eerie silence fell over my comms.

***

I stopped shooting at the same time that Jered did from behind me. Both sides of the conflict had us surrounded, and they stopped fighting each other for a moment. I reached over with my lower right arm and removed a device strapped to my left secondary arm. It was the detonator. I could feel Jered turn to face me. I pointed up to the stars.

***

Acheron warships were visible high above us, just bright lights that moved ever so slowly against the field of background stars. I looked down at Gaven and tried to peer inside his alien helmet. All I could see was my ghostly reflection in the polished black mirrors. Gaven activated the device, and a bright light lit the battlefield from above. The warships exploded in a blinding display of nuclear obliteration. Soldiers on both sides of the conflict looked up in unison, the explosions reflected on their faceplates.

As I stood there, staring at my friend in astonishment, debris from the exploding ships began raining down on the ice moon in a light show like nobody had ever witnessed. Gaven held out his free hand and I took it in a tight clasp. It was his way of saying goodbye, a final handshake, brother to brother. I shook Gaven's hand firmly as we again came under fire from the angered soldiers on both sides.

I took several shots to my legs and fell to the rubble as I returned fire. The nearest Elysian soldier was a tall, dark-faced man with officer bars. It was Lacithe, his face serene behind a rifle spewing flames of death at me.

Gaven's torso shielded me briefly, but the overwhelming firepower soon tore through my suit easily. I watched in wonder as my limbs were lazed off and my torso pierced through by white-hot radioactive rounds. Death was not as painful as I had thought it would be. *How perfect*, I thought, *that Morale Officer Lacithe was there to finish me off*. I fell back, looking up at Gaven as my friend was slowly cut down above me. My vision went dark as if someone had turned out the only light in the universe.

***

My suit began to crumble around me as I was drilled with fire from both sides. Pain ripped through me as I lost secondary and then primary arms. I fell backward over the lifeless body of Jered. I lay there staring glassy-eyed into the screens that showed the debris of my starships raining down in red and orange streaks like radioactive, fluorescent rain. Hacker and everything he had represented was gone. Below me was Jered's body. There was nobody left to save, not even myself.

***

Selina sat back in her seat with her eyes closed. The battle for Betwi-Three was underway as they sped back to Elysia. Morale Dispatches were announced over the ship's PA, recounting the battle's progress. Initial reports were cautious and offered few facts about who was winning. The other soldiers listened intently for news of the inevitable victory.

Selina knew their forces would win, but she also knew Jered was not coming home alive. Call it a gut feeling or a woman's intuition. She knew her baby's father would never live to see his child. That thought brought tears to her eyes that trickled down her cheeks. Never seeing Jered again filled her heart with regret and sadness.

He would have never tried to get himself killed, she knew, but at the same time, she understood that the government wouldn't allow him to survive the battle. She caressed the data fob in her pocket. It was her last piece of him, and after she turned the data over to the Peacers, she would keep it for the rest of her life.

Cheering startled her and forced her to open her eyes and wipe them dry. The battle was over, and the moon was now in the hands of the Elysian Army. Two view screens a few rows ahead of her showed orbital feeds of the battlefield below. The ground was ghostly white from snow, and burnt craters pockmarked the clean snow. Near the Acheron fort, she saw the remains of an exploded Elysian combat tank and hundreds of dead bodies from both armies radiating outward.

The feed was too far away to distinguish anything more than colors and shapes. The soldiers on the transfer ship were told that two enemy starships were destroyed during the battle, and the surviving Acheron Army fought hard until the bitter end. Patriotic music played over the PA as some soldiers sang a victory song together.

Selina could only stare at all the dead bodies on the ground. She knew they were all humans. It was no longer just a suspicion by the Peacers; it was a fact, and she would be the one to release that fact back home. The names of the fallen began to scroll down over the battlefield images like credits to a holo-drama. She read every one of them until she saw Jered's name. Her eyes welled up again, and she fell back into her chair to cry.

Elysia,
Two Years later
27

Hector and Trille returned to the war memorial on the anniversary of Jered's death on Betwi-Three. They took time out from their busy lives and purchased blue Morning Glory flowers to place on the monument wall, just like thousands of others had done. This tradition, which dates back to the beginning of the war, had become a symbol for those who had made the ultimate sacrifice.

The yellow ball of Suth One was shining high in the blue skies above them as she placed the flowers into the narrow slot next to Jared's placard. The flowers mirrored the sky with a yellow center and pale blue petals. There was only enough room for his name and the date of his birth and death on the circular chrome placard. Trille carried her firstborn child in her arms as she touched the warm metal nameplate and closed her pale eyes.

Jered represented her first love, and even after his death, she still held a special place in her heart for him. Hector was less enthusiastic about coming, but when she pressed him about it, he relented, citing strong memories of the old Jered he had grown up with. She knew he no longer missed his old friend or even cared much that he hadn't come back. She thought perhaps Hector knew that if Jered had survived the war, she would never have married Hector. She would hold

Jered's child in her arms, not Hector's.

Like many vets who came to the memorial, Hector wore a hat emblazoned with his unit's number and the Elysian Army logo. He was just a LIFO soldier - Last In and First Out, but that didn't matter to anyone who had survived the war. No matter how they served or how illustrious their service record was, a veteran was a veteran. War was the ultimate bonding experience for humans and an exclusive club for those who had survived it.

A crowd had started to gather around the monument behind Hector and Trille. They were a motley group wearing ragged clothes and sporting long, stringy hair. Some wore old, tattered uniform jackets from their service in the Elysian Army. They all wore emblems of the Peacer Movement: three circles—blue, silver, and red.

Hector immediately became edgy upon seeing them. He moved closer to his wife and baby and looked over his shoulder as if he expected a confrontation. Trille let go of the nameplate, opened her eyes, stepped back, and bumped into Hector.

She turned and saw the Peacers gathering quietly around the monument. One of them, a woman with gray hair, stepped towards them. Hector moved between her and Trille. She stopped and motioned to the wall with her head as if she wanted past them.

"Do I know you?" Hector asked. Her face was familiar, but he couldn't remember from where.

The woman smiled thinly. Her hair was adorned with blue and red flowers, and she wore a ragged white shirt with the Peacer logo. A small boy held her hand but stood reverently behind her.

"I was a member of Jered's platoon, First Army."

Hector looked aghast at her, "You were in the war?"

She nodded.

"How can you be with them? Doesn't his death mean anything to you?"

The woman shook her head and then looked up at Jered's nameplate. "It means everything to us," she said, pulling the boy closer. He was about two years old, with blonde hair and wide, blue eyes. Trille quickly realized the child was the spitting image of Jered.

"Thanks to Jered's efforts, the war may end one day."

"What are you saying? Are you accusing Jered of being a Peacer?"

The woman returned her attention to Hector, and her dark eyes narrowed. "I know you've seen the interview with the Acheron Army soldier."

Hector bristled, "Lies and fake accusations! Peacers staged that footage."

"Jered recorded that interview, and you know it. He hoped it would be enough evidence to stop the war. To stop the killing of fellow humans on Betweos."

Trille looked at the blonde child and started to cry. She got down to her knees and stared at the boy. "Hector, this is Jered's child."

Hector recoiled in disgust but knew instantly that it was true, as he recalled that fateful day when Jered had shown him the footage. "You're the person who corrupted Jered."

"I didn't corrupt him. His government corrupted him and you and everyone else at this monument. The war is a terrible lie, and Jered exposed the truth."

Hector was about to light into her but held back when he heard the Peacers start to sing an anti-war song.

Trille stood up and took a step closer to Selina. Her eyes showed anger and regret as she spat in Selina's face. This was the woman who had taken her man from her and turned him into a traitor. Selina didn't retaliate. She pulled up the bottom of her shirt and wiped her face. She was defiant but unwilling to escalate. Trille turned away, unable to even look at Selina anymore.

Selina stepped to the wall and placed a black metal bracket with three black circles around it over Jered's name placard. The Peace Brackets had started to appear all around the monument as some of the relatives of those who were killed woke up to the fact that the war had been a lie. It wasn't enough to sway public opinion of the war, but it was at least some progress in that direction. She placed a red chrysanthemum with a yellow center beside the blue flower.

The red flower was for Gaven and every Acheron soldier who had ever died in the war.

Hector started to remove the items, but Trille stopped him. As the Peacers approached, she begged him to leave. Hector snarled at the crowd and broke away from them with his family.

Selina and her child watched them go and then looked at the war monument. Physically, it was the same monument that had been there the day they left for war, but now it was becoming an anti-war monument. The armed figures were the same, but red chrysanthemums were beginning to appear all over one of the soldiers, and blue morning glories started to cover the other soldier as more and more people recognized the suffering that occurred on both sides during the long war.

Selina picked up her child and held him tightly in her arms. His eyes shined in the sunlight as a breeze blew back his bangs. His name was Jayce, which meant the healer. He was their future, and she would raise him to defy the war.